'So what is your proposition, Mr Dexter?'

'I'd like you to pose as my fiancée for a week, Miss Florey.'

Vivian, in the act of taking a sip of wine, choked on it. 'I thought...I thought,' she spluttered, 'you said this was a business meeting?'

'It is. I did say *pose*.' Lleyton looked amused. 'That's obviously surprised you.'

Vivian raised seriously wary hazel eyes to his. 'Would you care to explain why you want me to *pose* as your fiancée?'

Lindsay Armstrong was born in South Africa but now lives in Australia with her New Zealand-born husband and their five children. They have lived in nearly every state of Australia and tried their hand at some unusual occupations, such as farming and horse training—all grist to the mill for a writer! Lindsay started writing romances when their youngest child began school and she was left feeling at a loose end. She is still doing it and loving it.

Recent titles by the same author:

MARRIAGE ULTIMATUM
THE BRIDEGROOM'S DILEMMA
THE UNEXPECTED HUSBAND

THE HIRED FIANCÉE

BY

LINDSAY ARMSTRONG

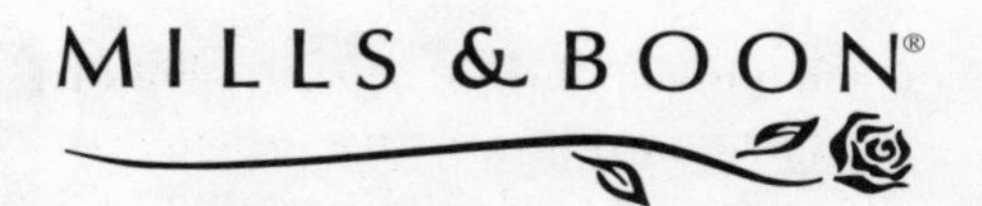

First published in Great Britain 2000
Harlequin Mills & Boon Limited,
Eton House, 18-24 Paradise Road, Richmond, Surrey TW9 1SR

ISBN 0 263 16622 8

Set in Times Roman 10½ on 12 pt.
07-0009-50644

Printed and bound in Great Britain
by Antony Rowe Ltd, Chippenham, Wiltshire

CHAPTER ONE

'NO GIRL wants to be the highest peach on the tree, where she can't be reached or squeezed,' Lleyton Dexter observed.

Vivian Florey drew a discreet breath to mask her inclination towards a more positive reaction. Such as leaning across his ridiculous glass desk and taking a well-aimed swipe at Lleyton Dexter's handsome jaw.

'Who said they did?' she murmured with great restraint, even managing to cross her legs negligently and lean back in her chair as if she was quite relaxed.

He had deep blue eyes, dark-fair hair and very white teeth, and his smile was a devastating mixture of wicked amusement and lazy worldliness. The rest of him, in stone chinos, a navy and maroon checked shirt and tweed jacket, was not unprepossessing either, although she'd expected him to be more formally dressed, as befitting the head of the Clover Corporation, a company that, amongst a great many other things, manufactured shampoo.

He was also a big man, tall, but streamlined, so you were aware of a subdued aura of power that was not unimpressive—unless you hated the man and Vivian was fairly sure now she did. Any man who referred to women as peaches to be squeezed deserved it.

Any man who was now subjecting her person to the thorough scrutiny he was subjecting it to was asking to be disliked and demolished. The only problem was she was not in a position to antagonise this man. The power of the Clover Corporation was very evident in this one office.

Not only did it boast sweeping views of the Gold Coast hinterland but it was some decorator's expensive dream. Heavy blue velvet curtains, white carpet, some exquisite paintings and *objets d'art*, as well as the vast glass-topped table on heavy carved marble piles that Lleyton Dexter used as a desk, with only a single slimline phone and a desk diary on it—and some glossy photos, but she'd brought those. Nothing so crass or commercial as a filing cabinet or even a computer was in evidence.

So she assumed a nonchalant air as that dense blue gaze travelled leisurely from her face and heavy corn-gold curly hair, down her figure, clad in a turquoise silk suit with a very short skirt, and down the length of her legs, in the sheerest of pale stockings, to her slender feet, all visible through the desktop.

That she happened to be shoeless at the moment was another annoying disadvantage she suffered. Why she happened to be shoeless was even more annoying.

She'd slipped her shoes off because they were killing her in the thickly carpeted lift on the way up to Lleyton Dexter's office, just for a moment's respite. But the lift had stopped abruptly between floors, the lights had gone out—and she had panicked. So that when it had resumed normal operations, only a moment or so later, and opened its doors at the right floor, she'd rushed out, weak and trembling with relief—without her shoes. The lift had gone on its merry way.

Frantic button-pressing had returned three of the other lifts to her, but not the one she'd been in. And for all she knew her beautiful but uncomfortable turquoise suede shoes that matched her suit exactly, were still riding up and down the building.

It had been bad enough—she was by then quite late—explaining all this to his receptionist. It had been sheer hell having to walk into this appointment in her stockinged feet and having to make the explanations again, this time to a man.

That was when he'd first directed that wicked smile at her, and she'd found herself wondering darkly whether behind that smile he'd been thinking— A real dizzy blonde, this one!

'Are you not suggesting with these images a sort of a pedestal impression, Miss Florey?' Lleyton Dexter enquired thoughtfully. He tapped the photo shots on his desk with a long forefinger.

'No. Yes. Look, it had never entered my mind,' she confessed, and frowned. 'I'm not quite sure what you meant in the first place about girls and peaches, Mr Dexter, but, believe me, Julianna Jones is delighted at the prospect of being the next Clover Girl.' She paused, leant over the desk and turned the photos round to face her. 'Does she look unhappy?'

'No,' he said slowly, 'but she looks unattainable. She looks a bit wooden to me, if you know what I mean. Beautiful, yes, but that spark of essential femininity seems to be lacking.'

'Because she's never been reached or squeezed,' Vivian couldn't help herself from commenting with some irony. 'Uh—' she gestured immediately to take the sting out of it '—her hair, on the other hand, is gorgeous. Believe me, ten girls out of ten would love to have her hair!'

Lleyton Dexter studied Julianna's river of smooth and shining dark hair meditatively for a long moment. Then he raised that worldly, wickedly amused gaze to Vivian, and subjected her to another thorough inspection.

This time Vivian found it curiously harder to maintain

her composure. This time she began to feel hot and bothered, and had the impression she wasn't hiding it too well. But that could have been because that lazy but all-seeing blue gaze seemed to have dispensed with her clothes, seen through her peach lingerie, and it now appeared that Lleyton Dexter was meditating upon her unclothed figure.

Then he shrugged casually. 'I think I'd rather have your hair in the ad, Miss Florey. As a matter of fact, I think you'd make the perfect Clover Girl.'

'Because I *do* look as if I've been reached and squeezed?' There was sincere outrage in Vivian's hazel eyes now. Not only because of his implication, not only because she resented being undressed mentally—although she did, and furiously—but also because of a strange little thrill of sensation running through her in response to his mental undressing of her. 'Mr Dexter—'

But after a light tap, the door to his office opened and his receptionist stuck her head around it. 'Excuse me,' she said, 'but concerning your shoes, Miss Florey—'

Vivian swung round eagerly. 'You've found them?'

'No, I am sorry. But the commissionaire's desk has checked all the lifts and enquired of all the offices in the building. No-one appears to have seen them.'

'So someone's taken them!' Vivian said incredulously. 'How could anyone do that? Oh, I hope they pinch *their* feet to death as much as they did mine!'

'One would have thought you might be relieved to see the last of them,' Lleyton Dexter murmured with utter false gravity.

Vivian swung round to face him. 'Very clever, Mr Dexter! The obvious problem, though, is how I'm going to go anywhere without shoes. One would have thought you might have considered that!' she parodied.

'If your car is in the parking ground I could arrange to

have it driven around to the front door. That's only a hop, skip and a jump from the lifts,' he offered.

'I didn't come by car,' Vivian said wearily. 'I came by train, then taxi.'

He raised his eyebrows, as if this was not only inexplicable but faintly ridiculous behaviour.

'The highway between Brisbane and the Gold Coast is such a mess these days, while they're widening it. You never know when you're going to be held up and the last thing I wanted to be was late. So the train seemed a viable option. In fact it was very pleasant—smooth, peaceful, and a much better option than battling with delays, detours and traffic jams,' she stated, through gritted teeth.

'May I make a suggestion?' The receptionist glanced at Lleyton Dexter and got a nod. 'Since it looks as if someone has pinched your shoes, I could send one of the girls out to buy you a pair, Miss Florey. Say, a neutral, inexpensive pair that would nevertheless get you home without further embarrassment?'

'Brilliant, Mrs Harper. Please do so right away. We will—er—foot the bill,' Lleyton Dexter added to Vivian.

'I can afford a pair of shoes—'

'No, no. If they were stolen in this building I feel it's the least we can do,' he assured her. 'What size shoe?'

'Six and a half, but look—'

Lleyton Dexter got up and walked round the desk to look at her feet instead. 'What would you suggest as a neutral colour, Mrs Harper?'

'Beige. Her bag is beige, so, yes, I think beige would be fine. Not too high. Would that have been the problem with your last pair, Miss Florey?' Mrs Harper enquired.

Vivian took an obviously deep breath this time, and suddenly dissolved into laughter. 'Talk about having a bad day! I can't remember a worse one. Look, thank you—

both. That is obviously the sensible solution but I insist on paying for them. I was the one who left them in the lift in the first place.' She reached for her bag.

'Not unless Mr Dexter changes his mind,' Mrs Harper murmured primly, and withdrew.

Lleyton Dexter returned to his chair, made a steeple of his hands and rested his chin on them.

Vivian closed her bag and put it on the floor. 'Does everyone do exactly as you tell them?'

'Quite often. Not always, of course, and not always *exactly* either, but—'

'Just—ninety-nine per cent of the time?' Vivian suggested.

'I get the feeling you could be the one per cent, Miss Florey.'

Vivian came back to earth with a bump and remembered the advertising agency she worked for and the significance of the Clover shampoo account, should it come their way. She dropped her gaze to the photos, and Julianna's smooth, beautiful features.

'The thing is,' she said earnestly, after a moment, 'OK, men may look at women differently, but it might surprise you to know that women dress mostly for other women. Also, it's women who buy your shampoo, and I really don't think they'd be put off by Julianna. However,' she conceded, 'now we know what you have in mind we could do things a bit differently. A fun type of shoot as opposed to drop-dead but possibly unattainably gorgeous.'

'Not yourself, however?' he enquired quizzically.

She opened her mouth to tell him not to start that again, but closed it with a snap that nearly dislocated her jaw. 'I've never modelled so I would come across as far more—wooden than Julianna, Mr Dexter. And she isn't really wooden, besides which it would break her heart—' She broke off and winced inwardly.

'Why don't you give it a whirl?'

She put her head to one side and frowned. 'You're not serious?'

'I am.'

'Why?'

'I like your style,' he said easily. 'By the way, may I take you to lunch? When your shoes arrive, naturally.'

Vivian mentally felt all around this surprising turn of events, as if searching for something that was going to jump out and bite her.

All of which Lleyton Dexter observed and found himself laughing inwardly. Five feet four, he judged, of sheer dynamite packed into Vivian Florey's slender frame. Was that what had prompted him to recite to her his diary's quote for the day about girls and peaches, which his eyes had just happened to fall upon? To get a rise out of her? Possibly. Then, of course, he'd had to come up with a qualification for that quote, which could, unfortunately, see the unknown Julianna Jones lose out on a job—although next to this girl she *did* look wooden, damn it!

'Lunch—where?' Vivian interrupted his slightly frustrated thoughts.

'There's very nice Italian restaurant across the road. I can vouch for the food and the ambience. I've also got a proposition to put to you, Miss Florey.'

Vivian blinked rapidly. 'Business or…?' She left it unsaid, although personal was clearly what she'd been thinking.

'Business, naturally,' he murmured, fixing her with a slightly sardonic gaze.

Vivian resolutely refused to blush. 'Forgive me,' she murmured back, 'but one never quite knows with men.'

'I'm sure,' he agreed seriously.

There was a moment's silence. Then, 'You're laughing at me!' she accused. 'You've been laughing at me since I first set foot inside this wretched office—OK, I must have looked pretty funny, but enough is enough!'

Another tap on the door saved Lleyton from having to reply. It was Mrs Harper again, with not one but three shoe boxes. 'I went myself,' she explained chattily. 'There's a little shoe shop just across the bridge on Chevron Island. And I got them on approval so you'd at least have a bit of choice, Miss Florey. Here we go.'

Vivian reined in her disgust of Lleyton Dexter, although breathing heavily again, and began to try on beige shoes.

'Walk around in them a bit,' Mrs Harper advised, 'before you make a choice.' And some minutes later she said, 'Well, that's my choice, for what it's worth, Miss Florey. That pair you've got on now. Neat, practical, but still stylish. What do you think, Mr Dexter?'

'Personally, I preferred the second pair. Perhaps not so practical, with the open backs, but they did suit her feet.'

Vivian stood in the middle of his office with her hands on her hips and wondered whether she'd strayed into a madhouse. Because he was doing it again, lying back in his chair and observing her as if there were only the two of them in the room, as if she were parading her body for him like some potential addition to his harem.

And not only that. He was contriving to make *her* aware of her body beneath the turquoise Thai silk suit, with its short sleeves and short skirt. It was a suit she'd always loved, not only for the colour but for its cut, and despite the short skirt—which was in vogue anyway, especially in a Queensland summer—it was not revealing, but plain and elegant and quite suitable for business. So how, she wondered, should it now suddenly acquire the ability to make her aware of the swell of her breasts beneath the top, the slenderness of her waist and the curve of her hips?

Because it wasn't the suit but Lleyton Dexter making her aware of these things, with the way he was watching her, she answered herself.

To make matters worse, although she knew he was doing it, there was also an impassive quality about him that seemed to denote a connoisseur of women who judged them on two standards alone: physical perfection and their performance in bed. To her horror, she could imagine herself being taken away to be bathed and groomed and perfumed, and then presented to him, all a-tremble with desire—the mere thought of which actually made her tremble inwardly, and hate herself for it.

But at least it enabled her to snap herself out of the trance he seemed to have put her in, without crossing her arms defensively over her body as she'd been strongly tempted to do—as if she had no clothes on—and even begin to wonder whether she was imagining it all.

'I'll take these, Mrs Harper,' she said definitely, and gestured down to the pair she was wearing. 'They're…they're the most comfortable of the three,' she said as she shot Lleyton Dexter a triumphant little glance. 'And thank you so much for going to such trouble. I really appreciate it,' she added warmly to Mrs Harper, 'but I must insist on paying for them.'

'Well, I'll leave you to sort that out with Mr Dexter.' Mrs Harper began to box the other pairs. 'Although they're already paid for at the shop. They were all the same price. I'll send these back straight away.'

Vivian sat down and reached once more for her bag, then her purse. 'I saw how much they were from the box so…' She counted out sixty-five dollars and ninety-five cents down to the last cent from her purse and laid the money on the desk.

But his phone rang, and it turned out to be at least a five minute call while she fidgeted and fingered the money, then rearranged the photos several times.

And after he'd finished the call, before he had a chance to say anything, Mrs Harper knocked and came in again, looking slightly crestfallen—and carrying a pair of turquoise suede shoes. 'Someone rescued them from the lift but didn't have time to take them down to the commissionaire until a few minutes ago,' she said agitatedly. 'And I've already sent the others back.'

Vivian closed her eyes, and said to the office at large, 'I need a drink, I think.'

'Let's go to lunch, then,' he murmured.

She opened her eyes and focused on him warily. 'I didn't say that.'

'We still have the proposition to discuss.'

She hesitated, then shrugged as she recalled her real purpose today: to bring home the Clover shampoo ad. It also occurred to her that she might be safer from whatever kind of electricity it was that Lleyton Dexter was capable of sending through her veins amongst a crowd. 'OK.'

The Evandale business area of Surfers Paradise, inhabited by a lot of legal and accounting firms amongst others, was not a large area, and there were some leafy areas and squares, and several colourful little restaurants. It was quite pleasant, Vivian reflected, as she looked around. The Nerang river flowed around the western side of the area and the Gold Coast City Council buildings, in park-like grounds and with an arts centre as well as a theatre, were across the road.

The restaurant of Lleyton Dexter's choice spilled out onto the pavement, surrounded by potted shrubs, and was bustling with life and colour and the delicious smell of food. There was a queue waiting to be seated, but Lleyton had been directed immediately to a table without having to join the queue. He'd ordered a bottle of wine, from which he now poured two glasses while they waited for their lunch.

'There. Cheers,' he said.

'Cheers.' Vivian took a sip and sighed with pleasure. 'That's a very nice wine. Would you believe anyone could have the kind of day I've had, Mr Dexter? Not that I want to start you off laughing at me again, but you have to admit, losing your shoes is traumatic to say the least.'

He grinned fleetingly. 'I do.'

Yes, that's it, Vivian thought to herself, a casual, friendly approach now, a bit of humour, and absolutely no reference to any kind of physical magnetic field that she was probably imagining anyway. 'So what's your proposition? Could I be forgiven for hoping it might improve my day?'

He directed her an amused little glance that seemed to say he was not in the least deceived. 'I'd like you to pose as my fiancée for a week, Miss Florey.'

Vivian, in the act of taking another sip of wine, choked on it. 'I thought...I thought,' she spluttered, 'you said this was business?'

'It is. I did say *pose*. Ah, thank you,' he murmured to the waiter as their lunch was put before them.

Vivian stared at the veal Ptarmigan she'd ordered, then raised seriously wary hazel eyes to his.

He looked amused. 'I've obviously surprised you.'

'Between you and your receptionist, grateful though I am to her, one could be forgiven for thinking one had fallen down Alice's rabbit hole. Not to mention your strange sentiments on women and peaches—yes, you have,' she said baldly.

'Ah, well, one day I might explain that to you. As for Mrs Harper, she's an excellent receptionist and she just adores—being helpful.'

'Would you care to explain why you want me to *pose* as your fiancée?'

'Sure. Don't let your meal get cold,' he advised. 'I'm going to be in a social situation for a week—not of my seeking, believe me—where I could become—well, prey to a variety of—women. With a fiancée by my side they'd have to hold off, wouldn't they?'

Vivian licked her lips and swallowed several times as she digested all this. 'Women make fools of themselves over you?' she hazarded after a long pause.

'I'm not sure why, but sadly, yes.'

'Not sure why,' she marvelled, and picked up her wine glass to cradle it with both hands. 'You don't think it has anything to do with being seriously wealthy, good-looking and in your prime?'

'If so, it didn't seem to make much of an impression on you. I could have sworn you barely contained yourself from slapping my face earlier.'

'You're right.' She looked at him broodingly and wondered why she had the distinct feeling she was being toyed with like the proverbial mouse. Although Lleyton Dexter didn't come across as any old cat, but a blue-eyed, sleek and deceptively mild tiger, toying with his prey. 'In fact I still don't approve of you at all, other than in a business context.'

'Wouldn't that make this an ideal partnership, then, for a week?' he suggested lazily. 'I mean, you wouldn't have the problem some others have, but you'd be the perfect buffer.'

'No.' She put her glass down and picked up her knife and fork. 'No, I couldn't do it. Are you crazy?' she added with a frown. 'And don't tell me you can't fend off women for yourself! You're big enough,' she added with irony.

He laughed aloud. 'No, I'm not normally crazy. Uh—how about if I said this Julianna Jones, in a more lively context, has my blessing and we'll…hand the Clover Wines contract over to your agency as well?'

Vivian stared at him with her lips parted.

'It would be a big account. We're thinking along the lines of new labels, as well as a whole new image, and we're going into the export market. Have I got it right that you have a partnership in the agency?'

'Yes,' she said hoarsely, 'well, only a ten per cent stake, but… But you didn't like my ideas for the shampoo ad so I'm confused.'

'If I hadn't set eyes on you I'd have probably been perfectly happy with them.'

Once again she could only stare at him.

'And I was very impressed with your firm's honey ad. That's why we got in touch. I believe you had a big part in that?'

'I…did,' she said feebly.

'And that you took honours in Graphic Design at university?'

'You do your homework well, Mr Dexter.'

'Would a week of your time be such an imposition in light of what you might gain from it, though?' he asked idly.

'But that's sheer bribery and corruption!'

'Well, it's a quid pro quo—'

'No!' Vivian interrupted. 'How on earth can I know what I'd be getting myself into? You could be…you could be anything!'

'I could, but I'm not. Let me tell you a few more details. My sister is getting married. The week leading up to these nuptials is to be spent in a frenzy of house parties and the like at the family estate. My mother will be in residence, as will a variety of others—you may never have to be alone with me if you don't want to. And my mother is a pillar of society, believe me.'

Vivian concentrated on her lunch but without tasting it. 'Is that how the rich and famous do it?' she commented eventually.

'Isn't that how most of us do it?' he countered.

'Not "on the family estate", believe *me*, Mr Dexter.'

'It'll be a fun time, Vivian,' he assured her.

'But we can't just *say* we're affianced without at least occasionally proving it,' she objected.

'I'd be perfectly happy to respect your wishes for no overt demonstrations of affection. We could make it known it's unofficial as yet.' He finished his lunch and tranquilly pushed his plate away.

'What about your mother and your sister? How would they react to you suddenly producing a perfectly strange, even if unofficial, fiancée?'

'My mother and sister generally go along with me.'

She made a frustrated little sound in her throat. 'I can imagine! But there's got to be—there's got to be something else behind this!'

'There is,' he said meditatively. 'I've discovered myself imbued with the idea of pushing myself up in your estimation.'

Vivian chewed her last mouthful carefully and put her knife and fork neatly side by side on her empty plate, then took a sip of water. All as a ploy to delay having to look into Lleyton Dexter's deep blue eyes. Because something had touched her strangely at his quiet words. That odd little frisson had run down her spine again. That meant what? she wondered. Surely she couldn't be seriously attracted in any way to the man, blast him?

She said at last, 'If *that's* so, what's wrong with conventional ways of trying to impress a girl, Mr Dexter? Rather than bribery.'

His blue gaze held hers. 'Two reasons, Vivian. I like a bit of a challenge these days… And I have the feeling you'd repel conventional tactics to the death. Speaking figuratively. Although,' he said softly, 'what you might do to promote your business is another matter.'

Vivian spoke without thinking, but right from the heart, 'A straight, honourable deal, Mr Dexter? Julianna Jones and Clover Wines for a week of only *posing* as your fiancée?'

He nodded.

'You're on,' she said.

'Vivi—how old are you?' Stan Goodman, senior partner of Goodman & Associates, said wearily the next morning.

'Twenty-five, Stan, going on twenty-six—as you know!'

'Isn't that a bit old to be falling for the three card trick?'

'I couldn't help myself,' Vivian said flatly. 'Besides, look what it's bringing to the firm!'

'And what happens if you don't only *pose* as Lleyton Dexter's fiancée, but end up in his bed, to put it brutally?' He looked at her over the top of his glasses.

'We didn't actually spell that out,' Vivian conceded, 'but if you think I can't resist some man for a week, Stan, you do me an injustice.'

'This is not just "some man", Vivi.'

She moved her shoulders restlessly. 'All right, he's got an awful lot going for him, but he managed to alienate me from the moment I set eyes on him. In fact, Lleyton Dexter may not know what he's let himself in for.'

Stan Goodman threw up his hands in despair. 'Don't,' he pleaded. 'If I can't persuade you to back out of this, promise you won't do something as silly as trying to give him a run for his money?'

Vivian hesitated, because while she knew Stan would be as good as his word, and not hold it against her if she backed out of Lleyton Dexter's proposition, she also knew the agency needed both Clover Shampoo and Wine. One of the senior partners had been lured to another firm only a few days ago and had taken some of their biggest accounts with him. It was the reason she hadn't walked out of Lleyton Dexter's office in her bare feet yesterday, after all, she mused. She knew that Stan, and the agency, had their backs to the wall at the moment, although she doubted Stan realised that she knew the full implications of that defection.

But she could see the effect it had had on him. He'd lost weight, he looked tired and not very well. On the other hand, she didn't want him to think she was going above and beyond the call of duty for the agency and therefore add to his problems so…

'Stan,' she said thoughtfully, 'I'm afraid it's about time somebody did. Trust me, though. I won't do it in a way to lose us the wines or the shampoo.'

'What about Ryan Dempsey?'

Vivian suffered a moment of incredulity, because she'd forgotten all about Ryan, who had also worked for Goodman & Associates. 'We, Ryan and I, are finished, as you know—it was over ages ago.'

Stan raised an eyebrow.

Vivian hesitated. 'I know what you're thinking. That he broke my heart. He didn't,' she said quietly, at last.

Stan, who was fifty, stared at the brightest star in his firmament, despite the trouble she was prone to attracting, and sighed inwardly—because he'd known Vivian Florey since a child and knew more about her than she might know about herself, he sometimes felt.

Richard Florey, Vivian's father, had been a good friend of his. And when her mother had died, when she was about six, her father had been brokenhearted. He'd never remarried and, as a civil engineer, had spent a lot of his life in remote locations, wherever possible having Vivian with him. At other times it had been boarding school for her, although Stan and his wife Isabelle had gone out of their way to visit her and have her home for weekends.

And, much as she'd hated to be parted from her beloved father, it had bred in Vivian a fear of commitment. The sense of loss that her father had carried to his grave had transmuted in his daughter to a wariness of letting anyone get that close to you, in case you lost them. The lifestyle hadn't helped either. Friends made had so often been left behind, and it had been the same with familiar environments. Then her father had died when she was eighteen, and the only relationship Stan had seen Vivian share with a man had reinforced her fear of commitment. Ryan Dempsey had walked out on her.

Not that she didn't have plenty of friends now; not that she hadn't made the most of her talents, with his help; not that she didn't have a busy, fulfilling lifestyle.

'Vivi,' he said slowly, 'have you ever considered that you tend to hold men, particularly, at arm's length?'

Vivian blinked. 'I…yes, Stan,' she said quietly. 'And I think I know why. The way I grew up—Dad and so on,

Ryan…and I *thank* you for worrying about it too.' She swallowed and cleared her throat and was suddenly all the more determined to bring Clover into the Goodman fold, because Stan had been a bit like a surrogate father to her and he'd certainly had a big hand in guiding her career.

She went on carefully, 'I guess I've thought it was something time would take care of, and I'm sure it will. But, honestly, I'm not that bothered about it.'

'All the same, I'd hate to see you get hurt again, and this—this is playing with fire.'

'Why? He can't be that irresistible!'

Stan only stared at her until Vivian subsided.

A few moments later she said, 'I think I know what you mean. If I wasn't the tiniest bit intrigued, I wouldn't have fallen for it. But, don't you see? That's all part of it, Stan. He…he played me like a fish on a line. And now he probably thinks he's got me reeled in. He hasn't, and he's going to find out why!'

'When do you go?' Stan asked with a sigh.

'In three days' time.' She told him the date on which she was to present herself once more at Lleyton Dexter's office. 'All kitted out for a bit of fun on the family estate,' she added with a grin, then frowned. 'Oh. I forgot to ask where it is!'

'I can tell you. On the Hawkesbury. About a hundred acres, I believe, with tennis courts, a pool, stables, their own private jetty, a croquet lawn, three houses on the estate—the main one being a two-storeyed yellow and white version of a southern plantation-style manor with twelve bedrooms. The estate is called Harvest Moon.'

Vivian started to laugh. 'Stan, if you were trying to overwhelm me there is something about me you may not know—I play a mean game of croquet. One of my schools taught me that, as well as tennis and how to ride horses.'

* * *

Two days later, however, she wasn't feeling as confident.

Her suitcase was open on her bed, piles of clothes surrounded it and her apartment in a high-rise complex on the Brisbane River was flooded with late-afternoon sunlight. She loved her apartment, she loved the river, the Storey Bridge she looked out towards, the walkway from the buildings to the Botanical Gardens, the cliffs on the opposite bank that were floodlit at night and the riverside cafés, restaurants and weekend markets.

She sighed as she looked at the chaos on her bed, and walked through to the lounge dining area with its panoramic views. She'd used lemons and greens as a colour scheme for this area: two plump settees covered in lemon cotton with green leaves and green piping, soft green carpet and a wrought-iron dining setting with a glass-topped table.

She paused at it and tapped the glass lightly with her fingertips, thinking as she did so of another glass-topped table. Was she being exceptionally foolish to participate in this charade? Should she, once she'd cooled down, have called it off?

She turned away and went to curl up on a lemon settee, remembering as she did so Stan's warnings to her, not only on the subject of Lleyton Dexter but on her own state of mind—as evidenced by the growing conviction, from the time she was eighteen, that she was a bit of a loner. Not so much that she didn't have friends, but emotional attachments were another matter—and that, of course, encompassed the area of men.

On the other hand, she thought, could it be that the right man simply had not appeared on her horizon? Ryan—well, yes, at the time she'd thought he was it. She winced inwardly as she remembered how she'd lowered her guard, how she'd allowed herself to assume she was over her fear of commitment and that they *would* commit. Only to discover that this man whom she'd thought she loved, and had certainly enjoyed being with, had not had the same agenda.

Fun, togetherness, a common interest, yes, but no ties had been what Ryan Dempsey had sought from her. And although it had hurt so much at the time, it had to be a lesson that would guard her against Lleyton Dexter if by some freakish turn of fate he turned out to be the right kind of man for her. Surely that experience would provide her with the sensory perception to know that she was playing with fire?

But how *could* he be the right kind of man? He was obviously disenchanted enough with love and romance to want a challenge to go with it; he'd said so quite openly. He had used bribery and corruption to reel her in… And knowing all this had to be a powerful reason to resist to the death the odd physical stirrings his sheer attractiveness seemed capable of producing, and give further cause to despise him.

All the same, there was nothing to prevent her from backing out of the deal, even at this late stage. Stan had made his position plain—he certainly wasn't egging her on to bring to Goodman & Associates the Clover wine account by this means. And she did have a number where she could reach Lleyton Dexter. They'd exchanged home phone numbers at their lunch. In case of any unforeseen circumstances, he'd said wryly, but with a little glint of sheer devilry in those blue eyes. So that she'd started to protest, then thought better of it.

And that number was still reposing in her diary, in her beige bag, which just happened to be sitting on a side table next to her settee, where there also just happened to be a cordless phone.

She reached for her bag, got the diary out, flipped through the pages, and had put her hand on the phone when it started to ring. She took her hand away, then picked it up.

'Hello? Vivian Florey.'

'Lleyton Dexter, here, Vivian.'

She froze and wondered how she could have forgotten how deep his voice was.

'Oh.' She licked her lips. 'Hi!'

'Just checking to see if our deal is still on. If you've got cold feet now's the time to let me know.'

She was silent for a long moment as a series of emotions rose within her. Annoyance that he should sound brisk, impersonal and businesslike, hackles rising at the "cold feet" implication, but also an urge to say simply, Yes, I have. She should have known what would win…

'No, Lleyton. I presume it's OK for me to call you that? No cold feet. How about you?'

He didn't respond to that. He said, 'Good. Look, I've had a slight change of plan. I'm in Brisbane and I plan to fly home from here tomorrow morning rather than Coolangatta. I thought it might be a good idea for us to have dinner tonight so I can fill you in on some family background. I can also pick you up first thing tomorrow morning and take you out to the airport.'

'Sounds…fine,' she said slowly, although she was thinking, Could this even be another escape hatch? 'Uh—I've still got to pack, so how about somewhere close to home for me, like the Riverside?'

'OK.' He named a restaurant—one of her favourites, with a verandah dining area overlooking the river. 'Let's say six-thirty. See you there.' The phone went dead.

Vivian looked at the receiver and was tempted to throw it across the room. She didn't, but any doubts she might have had about this man not requiring a goodly dose of his own medicine were laid to rest, she discovered.

He was already sitting at a table as she threaded her way through the throng of after-work drinkers and early diners, all taking advantage of a lovely Brisbane evening and the river.

And, unlike the previous occasion, he was very formally attired this time, in a lightweight grey suit, white shirt and navy tie. She'd chosen to be much more casual. Slim white trousers, a white voile blouse beautifully embroidered with seashells that just reached her slender midriff, hot pink mules and a matching raffia holdall. As usual her hair was a riot of curls and she wore no make-up, no nail varnish, no jewellery.

But she cut a swathe through the place, which Lleyton Dexter didn't fail to notice as she approached. And when she stopped at the table they simply stared into each other's eyes for a long, curiously fraught moment.

It struck Vivian that his dark blue eyes were expressionless, but his mouth was set in an oddly hard line. It also struck her that this was a different version of Lleyton Dexter, a long way from the wickedly amused, worldly but laid back version of the man she'd met two days ago. This man was all you might expect from the head of a vast corporation: not someone to be trifled with at all. The tiger was plain to be seen and not in a toying mood, she found herself thinking fancifully, although with an inward little tremor. But there was something else.

There was that magnetic intensity flowing between them again, despite that dispassionate gaze. Something like static electricity that kept her silent as they traded glances almost like blows.

Then she moved restlessly as she knew that there was

a sheer, stark physical appraisal going on between them. The kind that a man and a woman who found each other intriguing, despite their better judgement, exchanged. All the same, she couldn't break the contact.

He did. He stood up, smiled a little dryly at her and pulled out a chair. 'You're looking in holiday mode already, Vivian.'

'Thank you.' She sat down. 'You're not.'

He raised an eyebrow. 'I've been exceptionally busy. I'll wind down tomorrow. Will you have a drink?'

'If you're ordering wine, that's all I'll have.'

He signalled to a waiter and handed her a menu. She chose prawns Creole and a Greek salad, and after a moment's thought—and a raised eyebrow at her, to which she responded to telling him she could definitely recommend it—he ordered the same. When the waiter had departed, he pulled a grey velvet box from his jacket pocket and put it in front of her.

'Not—an engagement ring?' Her hazel eyes were supremely mocking as she raised them to him.

'A ring of some kind.'

Vivian managed to regulate her breathing through a sheer effort of will before it became apparent to anyone that she was wildly angry. She picked up the box and flipped it open. It was wideish platinum band with small baguette and brilliant cut diamonds running round it. In the middle was a square pink diamond, not large, but stunning in its colour and fire.

'Well, that's lovely, Lleyton,' she said, 'but since this is unofficial, I'll wear it on my right hand.' The ring fitted snugly, perhaps a little too snugly, and that told her it would fit her left hand perfectly. 'How did you know what size to buy?'

'I took a punt. I also mentioned your shoe size; that

seemed to help. But I'd rather you wore it on your left hand.'

'If wishes were horses, beggars might fly,' she murmured. 'Take it or leave it, Mr Dexter.'

'Because you believe in reserving your left hand for the real thing?'

'I do.'

'Has anyone suggested the real thing to you, Vivian?'

She raised her eyebrows. 'Proposed marriage, you mean? No. That doesn't mean to say it won't happen. How about you? Done any *real* proposing of your own lately, Lleyton?'

'No. That doesn't mean to say I haven't received a few…suggestions along marriage lines.'

'That's sad,' she said with a shrug. 'I mean never to know if they want you or your money. What you really need to do is fall in love with an heiress. If your fortune wasn't an issue you'd be in a better position to judge whether an unsatisfactory outcome was due to shortcomings in you yourself, perhaps.'

'Such as?'

The wine arrived at this deadly point in their conversation—and immediately diverted Vivian's attention. It was a Clover Riesling. 'Well,' she said, as she studied the bottle with its plain maroon label and gold lettering, 'conservative, fairly elegant—but deadly dull, if you don't mind me saying so.'

Lleyton Dexter blinked once. 'So, how do you like your men, Vivian?'

Her eyes left the bottle and widened on him. Then they began to dance with amusement, although she lowered her lashes immediately. 'Dashing Latin lovers are more my style, Lleyton. Especially with ponytails—and I don't mind the odd earring. I don't mind if they can cook, I love it if they're good dancers because I adore to dance myself, and flashy dressers—boy, can they give you a good time!'

He was silent, and when she looked across at him again his gaze was unimpressed and faintly sardonic. 'I gather you were talking about the Clover label, Vivian?'

She grinned. 'I was. Sorry—too good an opportunity to resist. But don't automatically discard Latin lovers, Lleyton, as my preference in men. By the way, I've had a few ideas for new labels. Like to see them?'

He nodded, and she delved into her holdall. A few minutes later, he lifted his head and said, 'You may just have redeemed yourself, Vivian Florey.'

CHAPTER TWO

SEVERAL expressions chased across Vivian's face, but the principal one was that of having the wind taken out her sails, although that followed her initial ire at having to redeem herself over anything.

'You like them?' She pointed to the three drawings on heavy parchment paper delicately coloured with pastels.

He studied them again. They were narrow and long, as if you were looking through a half-open door, and there was a couple in each one, a man and a girl. One of the couples was sitting on a wall with their arms around each other overlooking a poppy-studded field of golden corn. Her skirt was frothing out and he was all in black—and with a ponytail. The second had a couple holding hands, with the girl holding a cartwheel hat, next to a small white church with some tall, dark cypress trees beside it, and in the third the girl had her arms around the man's neck and they were kissing beside a stream.

She'd used colours such as violet, green-gold, chalk-blue and ruby. Running vertically beside them was the one word—CLOVER.

'I like them very much. What made you come up with them?'

She propped her chin on her hands. 'I was thinking about wine—really thinking about it, I mean. Thinking of it as a celebration of life, the earth, the sky, Mother Nature, but especially human emotions—that kind of thing. Which this label—' she sat back and flicked a finger at the Clover bottle on the table '—sort of denies. It takes itself so seriously. Almost to the point of losing the point. Wine should be drunk as a celebration. Of love.' She shrugged. 'Or a delicious meal, or only the fact that...' She paused.

'Go on.'

'You got it wrong and no one pinched your shoes after all!'

His eyes changed. Genuine amusement crept into them and then he started to laugh.

Vivian laughed too, and surprised herself by saying, 'That's better. Things were getting to shoot-out at the OK Corral stage a little earlier! Tell me about this family of yours I'm about to hoodwink.'

Their meals arrived, and it wasn't until they'd both tucked in that he said, 'My mother is probably the best place to start—my father died about ten years ago. She's a born upholder of moral values, a serious do-gooder, in that she supports several charities as well as being a very—vigorous, outspoken kind of person. Then there's Marguerite, my sister. She's thirty-two and marrying a guy called Eddie, and we call her Mag. Last but not least there's my younger brother Ralph, who has a tendency to be the black sheep of the family.'

Vivian shut her mouth with an audible click. 'In what way?'

'He's artistic.'

'There's nothing wrong with that,' Vivian protested.

'No,' Lleyton agreed a shade dryly, 'but when you run through the amount of money Ralph has in the pursuit of it...' He shrugged.

'What kind of art would we be talking about?'

'Music. Several highly unsuccessful rock bands.'

'Would I be right in assuming neither you nor your

father were artistic?' she enquired with a grin. 'And particularly not rock enthusiasts?'

Lleyton narrowed his eyes. 'Philistines bent on commerce and trade, in other words?'

'I didn't say that, but I've got the feeling poor Ralph might have been made to feel slightly inferior because he lacked your business acumen.'

Lleyton considered. 'You could be right. But Ralph is free to go his own way so far as I'm concerned.'

Vivian looked quizzical. 'That sounds fairly unenthusiastic and guarded, Lleyton, but—it's none of my business. How old is he?'

'Twenty-six.'

'And how old are you?' Vivian asked curiously.

'Thirty-five. Quite long in the tooth, in fact. You would be—twenty-four?'

'Twenty-five. Nearly twenty-six. Too young for you?'

'What makes you think that?' he asked.

'Don't know.' She shrugged. 'Just testing. You did ask me how I liked my men.'

'I thought I indicated during our last meeting that you didn't go against the grain of what might be acceptable to me in the feminine form.' He sat back and picked up his wine glass.

'When you say things like that, Lleyton Dexter—' Vivian stopped frustratedly.

He waited with one coolly raised eyebrow but she could swear he was laughing at her.

'You annoy the life out of me,' she said through gritted teeth. 'And you were the one who viewed me as some sort of—houri. Don't think I didn't pick up the vibes!'

'A temptation towards earthly delights one should be strong enough to resist?' he suggested. 'You got it in one, Vivian.'

She gasped. 'How can you sit there and admit that?'

'I guess I'm only human,' he murmured.

'That makes it even worse—look, if that's what you really think I am, and you want to back out, just say the word,' she commanded.

'I don't. Do you?'

Their gazes clashed, her hazel eyes fierce, his simply loaded with irony.

'If you're going to treat me like some sort of prostitute—if you're going to be superior and judgmental and all the rest,' she said scathingly, 'I—'

'My apologies. I won't do it again,' he said, and added, 'It would be a pity for your creative genius to lose out, though.'

Vivian switched her glance to the drawings.

'They're a little surprising, actually,' he drawled, following her gaze. 'Rather more romantic than one might expect from you, Vivian.'

'That's because you don't know me in the slightest,' she retorted, then flinched. 'That's what a creative force is about,' she amended. 'It's a feeling for...things, be they why people eat honey or drink wine.'

'Then you must have some sort of a feel for romance. But before we get back to the OK Corral—are we on or off?'

She opened her mouth, closed it as Stan Goodman's tired, strained face swam before her, then said carelessly, 'On, Mr Dexter. Which means I ought to go home and pack.' She pushed her plate away. 'I take it I should come prepared for...boating, tennis, horse-riding, even croquet—not to mention balls, soirées, luncheons and the like?'

'Who told you that?'

'My boss and senior partner, Stan Goodman. He got it

wrong? I never did ask him how he knew so much about Harvest Moon.'

'He got it right,' Lleyton Dexter remarked, and stood up.

Vivian followed suit and waited as a waiter rushed forward with the bill, then they walked out side by side.

'May I see you to your door?' he enquired.

'Oh, I'll be fine,' Vivian said. 'It's only a hop, skip and a jump from here…' She stopped, looking suddenly awkward.

'I wasn't proposing to force my way in to see your etchings, but I do need to know where to pick you up from tomorrow,' he murmured.

They were just about to step onto the Riverside walkway. It was dark now, but the lighting was sufficient for him to see the colour that came to her cheek. The way his lips twisted told her he had, and she immediately went on the defensive.

'How much is this worth?' She held up her right hand.

'About…' He shrugged. 'Sixty thousand dollars.'

Vivian tugged the ring off, hunted for the box in her holdall and handed both to him. 'You keep it. I've decided not to wear it.'

'Why?'

'I may have business reasons for doing this. I may even have been reeled in like a fish on a line.' Her eyes held his steadily. 'But I'd rather not have sixty thousand dollars of your wealth sitting on my person like a ball and chain.'

'Very eloquent.' He slipped the box into his pocket.

She sucked in a breath, then moved her shoulders and started to walk. 'Besides which I hardly ever wear jewellery, apart from my mother's pearls—and only those on very grand occasions. So I could easily lose it.'

'It's insured. By the way, the more you wear pearls next to your skin, the better it is for them,' he said.

'Thank you for that advice, but—' She stopped frustratedly. '—I'm really not a jewellery person, although I do have a sentimental attachment towards my mother's pearls.'

'I think pearls would look stunning against your skin, Vivian.'

She stopped walking again and faced him militantly, but he remained unabashed and pushed his hands casually into his trouser pockets.

'In fact,' he mused, 'I can almost see you in pearls and—nothing else.'

To her horror, a vision of herself welcoming Lleyton Dexter into her arms wearing nothing but pearls rose to her mind's eye and caused her to break out in a fine dew of sweat. Because it was happening again. Just by a choice of words. Well, pretty provocative words, she acknowledged. In fact so provocative she should have been annoyed and disgusted, and yet this man contrived to have the opposite effect on her.

Once again the mental undressing was not only his province. Once again she was hit by the impact of his wide, strong shoulders beneath his jacket, how tall he was and how rather breathtakingly magnificent, as many of the arrested glances of the women they'd passed on the way out of the restaurant had confirmed.

'I thought we'd agreed that kind of talk was out?' she said tautly.

'We agreed I wasn't to make you feel like a prostitute or some kind of houri, but that was a genuine sentiment. Because, Vivian,' he said softly but pointedly, 'we can't help thinking of each other in those terms. It's...' He shrugged. 'It's there, between us.'

'Do you think so?' she countered. 'I very much suspect, on the other hand, that it was to pay me back for rejecting your r-ring,' she said caustically, although her voice let her down and wobbled slightly. 'And I consider it in bad taste and hitting below the belt!'

He grinned a shade satanically. 'Well, only if it hit home.'

She set her teeth and closed her eyes briefly in rather revealing embarrassment.

'But I also thought you enjoyed a contest, Vivian,' he added lazily.

'You thought wrong. At least, that's getting too personal,' she warned. 'What was I saying before you—'

'Told you my inner thoughts?' he supplied blandly. 'It was to do with why you won't wear my ring.'

She shot him a scathing look and started to walk again, swinging her bag. 'That's right. I was going to say that the fact that I don't wear jewellery could account for the reason you've held off buying me a ring!'

'I'll certainly use that as an explanation should anyone comment on it.'

She looked up at him and suddenly burst out, 'Damn it, did you go out and buy it especially for me or…what?' She stopped abruptly, because the words had come out without her realising that, subconsciously, this must have been tantalising her.

His deep blue eye were severely enigmatic. 'If you ever decide to wear it, Vivian, I'll tell you then.'

The next morning Vivian stood in the hallway of her apartment with her bags at her feet and studied herself in the wall mirror.

She wore cream trousers, a cream blouse and had a navy jacket to hand. Her hair, freshly washed and cut in a bob to her shoulders, was all golden and curly, and she was blessed with long lashes which she had dyed several shades darker. It was her only concession to make-up. The darker colour seemed to bring up the greeny-gold glints in her eyes as well as accentuate them and she could never be bothered with mascara or spiky, sticking together lashes. And her skin was smooth and peachy, so she only used a moisturiser and a lipgloss.

Her lack of interest in make-up didn't extend to clothes, however. Her trousers were beautifully cut, so was the jacket, and the round-necked, short-sleeved blouse was divine. Her ankle boots were the finest Italian design and leather—a wonderful investment, because they weren't new by any means but still looked it. And it took a master cutter to tame her hair into the casual curls that she wore tucked behind her ear on one side so that it looked so natural.

All in all, she thought, not even the slightly weird but undeniably wealthy mob at Harvest Moon could find much amiss with her presentation. So what was troubling her about it?

She sat down on her suitcase and admitted to herself it wasn't her outward presentation but her inner fortitude that might be the problem. She'd been annoyed enough with Lleyton Dexter the previous evening to make this a breeze, one would have thought. But just before they'd parted in the luxurious foyer of her building something else had touched her.

Something that had held her silent and unable to think of a thing to say. Because she'd been struck by curiosity—what kind of a man was he really? she'd found herself wondering. What lay behind the two faces *he* could present? That touch of steel that had manifested itself as opposed to the—mocking, yes, but much more relaxed man of their first meeting. The sheer presence of him, in this mode, that made her feel as if she was tangling with a force that might be a bit much for her.

Or was it something else—the undoubtedly physical magnetism that did seem be reaching her, despite her protestations to the contrary to all and sundry?

She'd shivered suddenly, then rushed into speech. 'Well, here we are. I could be waiting here for you tomorrow if you let me know what time.'

He'd had his hands in his trouser pockets again and had simply watched her thoughtfully for a long moment. A tall, physically awesome man who would stand out from the crowd anywhere, in a superb grey suit and with an aura of authority and power from his broad shoulders down to his well-polished black shoes. Whereas she had suddenly felt rather small and vulnerable, rather exposed beneath his blue gaze that told her nothing—although it—rested squarely on her breasts beneath the voile, damn it!

'I'm not sure exactly what time but it'll be around seven. Why don't I buzz you?' he'd suggested at last.

'Good thinking. See you, then. And thanks for dinner!' She hadn't bothered with the lift but had gone through a doorway without looking back.

And all these thoughts had continued to plague her throughout a restless night, she acknowledged now, as she sat on her suitcase with her stomach in something of a knot. Up until now, she reflected, she'd got to like several men way before getting to the point of starting to think about them in a more-than-friendship context—then taken fright and backed away. It had been the same with Ryan. She'd got to like him a lot before becoming aware that she could also love him.

But she'd never been physically conscious of a man she'd only met twice, the way she was with Lleyton

Dexter. It was a new and disturbing experience, and to lie awake for hours with him on her mind and this strange reaction, this mixture of attraction and waging a war was, to say the least, unsettling. This *feeling*, she thought intensely, that they were a man and a woman who had a very adult and dangerous effect on each other above all else was mystifying. For her, Vivian Florey, anyway.

Then her eyes widened suddenly as something fell into place for her. It might be mystifying and dangerous for her, but was it, so to speak, all in a day's work for Lleyton Dexter? And she realised it was something that had plagued her from the start—he knew the effect he had on women, and he could virtually pick or choose amongst them for as long or as little as it suited him.

But knowing that on an intellectual level, she acknowledged, was not the same thing as finding oneself responding to it. So, how to protect yourself from him? How to banish those images he created so effectively, of being in his arms, of being a temptation towards earthly delight, being *the* one he couldn't walk away from?

Her buzzer sounded, and when she flicked it on she could see Lleyton Dexter in the outer foyer on her small security screen. 'I…I'm on my way down. Come in—won't be a minute.' She flicked the switch to release the doors to the inner foyer and turned the security screen off.

She also stood stock still, counted to twenty, then started to wheel her luggage to the door.

When the lift opened on the ground floor, she pushed the suitcase out swiftly and followed precipitately with her hand luggage and purse, almost cannoning into Lleyton Dexter.

'Oh, sorry,' she said breathlessly.

'That's all right—although I've never before been virtually mown down by a flying suitcase on wheels.'

'I…don't like lifts,' she confessed. 'And even more so after what *your* lift did to me.'

'Why on earth do you live in a high-rise building. then?'

Vivian shrugged. 'I only live on the third floor. I like the security, not to mention the views, and I use the stairs most of the time. Great for the figure.'

Lleyton Dexter's glance skimmed down her figure. 'I have to agree,' he murmured. He wore khaki trousers and a blue and white checked shirt with button-down pockets and the sleeves rolled up. 'By the way, I'm parked right outside the front door so we ought not to loiter.'

'Goodness me, no! That is definitely a no-parking area,' she told him severely. Then her expression changed as the front doors came into view and, beyond them, a silver-grey Rolls-Royce. 'On the other hand, I'm sure they'd make exceptions for that—not that I approve!'

'I won't do it again,' he promised as they went through the doors and down the shallow steps. He opened the front door courteously for her before dealing with her bags, then slid in beside her. 'Great day for flying,' he remarked, as he steered the big car into the street.

'Yes, thank goodness,' she answered, leaning forward to look up at a clear blue sky.

'So you only use lifts when you have things to carry?'

Vivian settled herself back and couldn't help but be impressed by the comfort and luxury of the interior of the car. 'Of course not. I'm not that good a stair-climber, so in business and at other times I have to take them. But at home I usually walk. The building manager is also very sweet. When I've got groceries and things I just leave them in his office area on a little trolley and he brings them up for me. He's generally up and down all day. I don't really like heights either,' she told him casually, and started to do certain exercises, which kept her quiet for most of the rest of the journey to the airport.

He didn't seem to be put off by her silence. In fact he took two mobile phone calls on the way, so it wasn't that noticeable—or so she hoped, as she concentrated on relaxing herself. It was also a Saturday and, being so early, the traffic was light and the trip to Eagle Farm swift.

But she did speak suddenly as he bypassed the domestic terminal turn-off. 'I think you missed the turn.'

He glanced at her. 'No. We're going to general aviation.'

'You don't mean...' she swallowed suddenly. 'Not a commercial flight?'

'I do.' He drove the Rolls through a series of manned wire gates to finally pull up beside a hangar outside of which stood a lone light plane.

'You're not serious!' Vivian flinched as her voice rose to a slight squeak.

He frowned at her. 'I—am. I'm flying us down to Harvest Moon in that plane. Believe me, it's the best way to go. It cuts down the driving time at the other end significantly, and—'

'It may be the best way for you to go,' she said jerkily, 'but not for me!'

'Vivian,' he said patiently, 'I went from school into the airforce and I stayed there for many years. I can actually fly much bigger, much more complicated planes—'

'You don't understand,' she broke in earnestly. 'What do you think I've been doing for the last twenty minutes?'

'What? You've been rather quiet, but—I have no idea.'

'My *exercises*,' she said intensely. 'I told you I didn't

like heights—well, I hate flying as well! I have to go through a series of relaxation exercises every time I get on a plane. I can do it on a commercial jet now, thanks to help from a psychologist, but I could not possibly step aboard that flimsy little thing!' She pointed dramatically.

There was a moment's dead silence. Then he started to laugh softly.

'If you think it's funny—' she said fiercely.

'Vivian, that is *not* a flimsy little thing. It can seat six and it's very fast and a marvel of modern technology. Uh—well, yes, I am laughing,' he conceded, 'but mainly because I'm thinking along the lines of…the best laid plans of mice and men. Sorry.' He sobered. 'Uh—lifts, heights and now planes. And I thought you were such a modern girl.'

'I am, mostly,' she said gloomily.

'Sure there's nothing else you have a phobia about? Just so I don't make this kind of mistake again.'

'No.' She looked at him bitterly.

'OK. Then let's see what I can do to retrieve this.'

'I am not—'

'Bear with me, Vivian.'

Half an hour later she was seated beside him in the cockpit.

How he'd achieved it was impressive although she still hadn't got to the stage of being able to acknowledge that with any pleasure.

First of all he'd introduced her to the mechanics who looked after the plane and they'd given her a guided tour, little of which she'd understood, but it was hard not to be reluctantly impressed by their obvious expertise and enthusiasm for the machine. That was without even stepping aboard. Then there was the respect they had for Lleyton

Dexter. And there was his subtly different attitude towards her.

None of the tensions between them were allowed to surface. Nor was any reference made to her fear of flying. She was treated as an adult and a friend.

'OK?' he said, as they started to taxi towards the runway. She had on a set of headphones and he'd shown her how to avoid the mike when they were talking but still listen to the tower. He'd also shown her how to direct cool air onto her face.

'I....' She shrugged.

'Don't forget, I know what I'm doing, and you didn't seem to mind driving in a car with me—I'm no more of a risk-taker in a plane than I am in a car. In other words, my *own* safety is as paramount to me as yours.'

Vivian swallowed, and nodded.

'Besides which, you're in for a treat. It's a lovely day to be flying over Moreton Bay.'

It was. He pointed out St Helena and Mud Islands, Moreton Island, North Stradbroke and Peel, then they flew down the coast past Surfers Paradise.

And gradually she began to relax a bit. Not entirely—she doubted whether she ever would be able to—but it was a smooth flight and she lost the tendency to clutch at her knees whenever he banked. He also made it interesting by pointing out towns and rivers along the coast of New South Wales, explaining different instruments, thermals and the basics of flying. And a few hours later they were gliding over the Hawkesbury River with its wide mouth, then steep, deeply wooded banks, and he told her they were coming in to land on the private strip at Harvest Moon.

She immediately started to sweat again, and couldn't

concentrate on the above-ground tour he gave her of the property. Then he touched the plane down as lightly as the proverbial feather and rolled it neatly to a stop three-quarters of the way down the runway. And all her muscles had a tendency to want to dissolve, so that he had to help her down the stairs onto the ground.

He must have realised this, because he didn't let go of her hand as he said gently, 'That was extraordinarily brave of you, Vivian.'

A rush of delight ran through her. But it was followed almost immediately by a feeling she knew all too well.

'Lleyton, sorry,' she said in a muffled voice, 'but I'm about to be extremely sick.'

'Vivian, no.' He put his arms around her. 'You're not going to be sick. Take some deep breaths.'

'You can't stop it, Lleyton—'

'Yes, I can. Just do as you're told,' he said quietly but authoritatively. 'Breathe in. Don't forget you're on the ground now, and the air is fresh and clear. You're not alone and I'm full of admiration for you. Breathe in again.'

The quiet, confident way he spoke was incredibly soothing, she found to her astonishment. But, not only that, having his arms around her created a feeling of safety. A feeling of protection she hadn't known since her father had passed away, but different. And she breathed in and out deeply until the nausea passed.

'I don't know how you did that,' she said with a trace of wonder.

He smiled down at her and her heart tripped lightly. 'It was reaction more than motion sickness, I would imagine.'

'It must have been. It was,' she said ruefully. 'I often

feel nauseous when I get tense—or I get hiccups at the most awkward times!'

'You do have one or two problems, don't you, Vivian?' he murmured wryly. 'I know you haven't had hiccups in my presence, but have I ever made you feel sick—apart from insisting you fly with me?'

'Well, no,' she said slowly, 'and that's rather strange, because you've—at times you've produced some strange reactions in me.'

'Such as?' One of his eyebrows quirked as he looked at her quizzically.

She frowned and wished that she could hide from that all-seeing deep blue gaze, but that was part of the problem, of course. The forbidden attraction of Lleyton Dexter, and why, for example, she could be standing in the circle of his arms, having started out feeling safe and protected and rescued from making a fool of herself, but now feeling differently.

As in all too aware of him—from the magnetic power of his eyes, the way his hair lay, the lines of his face that could project wicked amusement or laid-back humour but at other times power and cool authority, to a physique that kindled her imagination. Because he was lean and strong and rather beautifully made and she felt petite and disturbingly feminine in his arms. Or aroused, she thought with a certain bleak honesty.

As in aware of herself, as his gaze travelled to her mouth, down the column of her neck and down her figure. Aware of a purely physical thrill to think that she could be desirable to him, that her body might tempt him; aware of things she might do, things drawn from her feminine psyche that she'd never explored before because no man had made her feel quite like this. And it was scary, but impossible to resist in spite of what she'd discussed with herself before leaving her flat…

She knew in the second before he did it that he'd guessed what was going through her mind. Or perhaps her body had spoken for her and he'd felt the fine trembling that had broken out all over her. But she knew that he would kiss her and she wouldn't have the will-power to stop him—that she'd answered his question much more effectively than she'd ever planned to do with words.

A few minutes later she stood quivering in his arms, her forehead resting against his shoulder, still aroused and breathing deeply as he ran his fingers through her hair and held her close to him. But just as she thought she was brave enough to let him see her eyes without giving herself away completely, a voice said, 'Pardon me.'

She would have jumped off the ground at this strange voice talking over Lleyton's shoulder, if she hadn't been so firmly anchored in Lleyton Dexter's arms. But Lleyton himself took his time about releasing her, and kept her hand in his as he turned to see who had arrived unannounced and unheard.

It was a tall young man, with dark hair in a ponytail, one silver earring, grey eyes, and he was leaning back against the bonnet of a Land Rover. She looked about wildly and coloured, because whoever he was he'd driven right up to the plane virtually without her being aware of it.

He straightened and bowed towards her. 'My apologies, ma'am, but I was deputised to come and pick you and Lleyton up after he buzzed the house.'

'Thank you, Ralph,' Lleyton drawled, still holding Vivian's hand, although she'd moved convulsively. 'May I introduce my fiancée, Vivian Florey?'

'*What?*' Ralph said blankly.

'You heard,' Lleyton murmured. 'Vivian, this is my brother Ralph. I told you a bit about him.'

'Yes. Yes,' was all she could say, because she was thinking all sorts of things. For one thing, when she'd been describing her ''Latin lover'' the previous evening she might just as well have been describing Ralph Dexter. For another, why should he be totally floored by Lleyton's introduction? So much that he still seemed to be struck speechless. Had Lleyton not told anyone he was bringing a partner at least? It was obvious he hadn't mentioned a fiancée…

And, on top of it all, how could she have got so carried away that she hadn't even heard him arrive? And, perhaps more importantly, had Lleyton been as unaware as she had? Or had he used the opportunity to cement the charade they were about to star in?

'Give us a hand with the bags, mate,' Lleyton said then.

Ralph sprang out of his open-mouthed daze. 'Sure. But first things first. Vivian! I like it. I like everything about you, to be honest!' He extended his hand with a boyish grin. 'Welcome to headquarters! This…is going to be quite a week.'

Vivian shook the extended hand, smiling feebly, she felt. 'Thank you. It…it looks lovely.' She really looked around for the first time, but there was not a lot to see. A concrete runway with a windsock and a small hangar at one end and virgin bush surrounding it, which made her feel even more foolish.

'I quite understand,' Ralph said with a wink. 'We're a mile from the house. Things do improve.'

'I imagine lunch is waiting,' Lleyton said a shade dryly.

Ralph lifted her bag out of the hold. 'So it is. It's a cardinal sin to be late for meals, Vivian, so you hop in the front and I'll help with the rest of the bags.'

But it was Lleyton who commandeered the driver's seat and Ralph who ended up sitting in the back, looking mournful.

'Who's here?' Lleyton asked.

'Mag and Eddie, Lady Wainright…' He paused with a grin as Lleyton swore. 'A couple of bridesmaids, our cousin Mary with her exhausting offspring and—Virginia.'

There was an odd little silence, then Lleyton said casually, 'Oh, well, we'll have enough for a four-ball after lunch. Unless—do you play golf, Vivian?'

'No. Tennis and croquet—'

Both Ralph and Lleyton groaned.

'But not golf. I do ride and swim, though,' Vivian offered.

Ralph, who was sitting forward in the middle of the back seat so his head was almost level with theirs in the gap between the front seats, said to his brother with a frown. 'You, a two-handicapper, don't know whether she plays golf?'

Vivian flinched inwardly.

But Lleyton replied tranquilly, 'Funnily enough, it just hasn't come up.'

Ralph grinned his boyish little grin, but this time it was knowing. Then he sobered to enquire, 'How long *have* you two known each other?'

'Long enough. There's the main house, Vivian. Straight out of *Gone With The Wind*.'

It was, but it was also lovely, Vivian decided. Set on a gentle rise, with sweeping lawns down to the river and a jetty, it was two-storeyed, the walls were a soft creamy yellow and the woodwork white. A verandah ran around the top floor, partly shading a broad, stone-flagged terrace on the ground, and there were flowering creepers growing up the verandah posts: port wine magnolia, jasmine and allamanda.

There was also, Vivian observed as the Land Rover drew up, a large party seated at a refectory-like table on the terrace—at lunch. She closed her eyes briefly and wished she were a thousand miles away, not to mention having had the sense *not* to touch Lleyton Dexter's proposition with a bargepole.

'Do you think,' she said involuntarily, 'it might be a good idea not to break it to them right away?'

'A very good idea,' Ralph said promptly. 'Setting the cat amongst the pigeons would be mild compared to the kind of disturbance you're liable to create with this news.'

'Thank you for your advice, Ralphie,' Lleyton drawled, 'but I'll handle it.' He shot his brother an old-fashioned look and turned back to Vivian. 'Compared to what you've achieved today, this will be a breeze.'

For an instant, as his deep blue eyes rested on her with a spark of amusement and also warmth, and her heart started to beat a most strange little tattoo, she wondered wildly whether she'd gone over some edge and this was actually for real—an engagement to Lleyton Dexter?

She licked her lips. 'I…I'm not sure about that.'

'Trust me,' he advised, and got out of the car.

The next ten minutes or so were incredibly confusing. It seemed Lleyton had not told anyone he was bringing a partner, let alone a fiancée—not that he divulged that titbit, and not, she had the distinct feeling, that he was heeding Ralph's advice. There was just an aura, despite everyone's surprise, that no one took issue with what he did at Harvest Moon.

Not even his mother. Although she did say, 'What's this? Lleyton, you might have told me you were bringing a friend! My dear, forgive me,' she went on to Vivian. 'not that there's any problem about Lleyton bringing a friend, but I could have had a room ready for you—unless you aren't staying?'

Amelia Dexter was something of a surprise. Very tall and slim, with copper hair cut in boy's cap, she was beautifully dressed in skin-tight jeans, a dazzling starched white blouse with navy butterflies and an awesome selection of gold chains and diamond rings. She was also exquisitely groomed and expertly made up.

Vivian, who had been expecting something quite different, forcibly stopped herself blinking. 'Uh—I was under the impression I was, Mrs Dexter, but I didn't expect you not to know about it.'

'Lleyton is a law unto himself, I'm afraid,' his mother said, with palpable resignation. She and her son exchanged glances. 'However, you are most welcome! What do we call you?' she added jovially.

'Vivian,' Lleyton said, before Vivian could open her mouth. 'Vivian Florey.' And he proceeded to introduce everyone around the table. 'By the way, we're parched and starved,' he added, pulling out one of the two free chairs for Vivian and sitting down himself in the other.

Causing Ralph to say with amusement, 'I'll get myself another one, mate.'

And so lunch resumed, with Vivian conscious of many impressions. That Lady Wainright was Amelia's oldest and dearest friend and possessed of a haughty languor that didn't always hide a sharp brain and a penchant for cutting comments. That the bride-to-be, Marguerite, was a raving beauty who was obviously fond of her brother and was marrying the rather quiet, unassuming man they all called Eddie. That Lleyton's cousin Mary did not have her 'exhausting offspring' around but looked thoroughly tired out. The two bridesmaids were also introduced. That left one other person at the table. Virginia Deacon, she'd been introduced as, but no one had explained her connection to the family or the wedding. Then it slowly dawned on Vivian that everyone was making a bit of a fuss of this Virginia, who was about thirty, she judged, and another raving beauty—although where Mag was dark-fair, like her brother, this girl was Nordic fair, with ice-blue eyes and the most delicate skin.

Was she sick? Vivian found herself wondering. She was certainly pale, although quite composed, if a little quiet.

It was Lady Wainright who put an end to the mystery as the main course of seafood and salad was removed and a dessert of orange segments in Cognac swirled with cream and sprinkled with chopped, roasted macadamia nuts was served.

She picked up her wine glass and said, boredly, 'Let's not pussyfoot around. I take it then it's definitely out with Virginia and in with Vivian, Lleyton? What a coincidence—two Vs.'

'Marlene!' Amelia stared at her best friend in outrage as a deathly silence reigned.

Marlene shrugged. 'I am his godmother.'

Lleyton spoke quietly, and directly to Virginia Deacon. 'We've been history for quite a while, haven't we, Ginny? Don't let them harass you or try to make mischief.'

Vivian switched her wide-eyed gaze to the other girl, and realised her mouth was open, but she seemed unable to shut it.

'If I remember correctly, Lleyton, I was the one who gave you your marching orders,' Ginny Deacon said to her wine glass, then raised those stunning pale blue eyes to his. 'Don't worry, I won't. Are…any congratulations due?'

'It's unofficial as yet.'

'What?' This time it was Amelia who uttered that single word in utter, blank surprise.

'Told you,' Ralph murmured, to no one in particular.

'You should have told *me*!'

Lunch was over and they were strolling towards the jetty, she and Lleyton, in lovely sunshine, with thick, well-tended lawn beneath their feet and the magic vista of a wide, curving river rippling along between Harvest Moon and hot, still, virgin bush on the opposite bank.

The lunch party had broken up in different directions. Amelia had offered to show Vivian her room, but Lleyton had said they'd have a walk first.

Now, when he didn't respond, Vivian stopped walking and faced him determinedly. 'Not only should you have told me it was one particular woman you were trying to fend off, Lleyton Dexter, but you should have told them to expect me! Or do you enjoy embarrassing not to mention humiliating people?'

'It's got nothing to do with anyone else but us, Vivian,' he said mildly, and, taking her hand, started to walk again so she had no choice but to follow.

It didn't stop her from saying vigorously, 'Rubbish! They're your family. This is to be a special occasion. But you've thrown them into turmoil. As well as putting me in a…in an unbelievable situation. I was starting to quite like you, but now…' She shook her head.

They'd reached the jetty and were strolling along it. 'I'd noticed that,' he murmured.

She frowned at him. 'What?'

He glanced down at her with all the considerable devilry he was capable of glinting in those deep blue eyes. 'How you'd started to like me, Vivian.'

She stopped abruptly, and not only because they'd reached the end of the jetty. 'That was…that was different.'

'Oh? How so?'

She shrugged a little helplessly. 'It was all bound up with surviving that flight without having made a complete fool of myself.'

'A celebration of your courage—that kind of thing?' he suggested.

She looked at him broodingly. 'Well, it was!'

'Are you saying whomever I'd been—short, fat, balding, middle-aged—you would have kissed me with sensuality and physical rapture?'

She pulled her hand away and stepped onto the wooden coping at the very edge of the jetty. There was a sleek power boat capable of seating quite a few people tied up to one side of it, a smaller one, and a catamaran tied to the other side as well as a jet-ski.

'Careful, Vivian,' he warned, and added, 'Aren't you going to answer the question—or can't you?'

She turned to him frustratedly. 'It doesn't change any of this, Lleyton!' She waved a hand towards the house. 'It—'

'Hang on,' he interrupted. 'Let's take one thing at a time. Why did you kiss me the way you did? I must tell you there seemed to be a certain voyage-of-discovery aspect to it for you—do you have to stand there teetering on the edge like that?' he added.

'I'm fine. I want to stand here and it's not one of my phobias,' she shot back. 'I have a good sense of balance.'

'Then how about applying it to what happened when we got off the plane,' he retorted.

Vivian put her curly head to one side and regarded him with all the falsely assumed patience *she* was capable of—like someone dealing with an inferior intellect. 'OK, if you really want me to. I don't like being kissed normally. In fact I've been known to avoid it like the plague! Even with men I've liked a lot more than you, Mr Dexter. So what does that tell us? It—'

'Vivian—'

'No, Lleyton, you asked for this. Of course we need also to put it into context. I was quivering like a jelly inside but also wildly elated, and, yes, you managed to achieve that. But as to the actual kissing—you're obviously an expert. Now that I'm beginning to understand why, I'm a lot less enthusiastic about it, believe me.'

'What the hell is that supposed to mean?' he queried with a certain rough impatience of his own.

Vivian opened her eyes at him. 'How can you say that when you have an ex-girlfriend sitting up there—' again she gestured towards the house '—obviously pining away for you, and you've got me in tow as a prospective new girlfriend not to mention fiancée? Forgive me, but I'm starting to buy the ''straight and honourable deal'' aspect less and less—'

'She's not an ex-girlfriend, Vivian. She's my ex-wife.'

In her extreme surprise, Vivian took an unguarded step backwards, and fell into the river.

CHAPTER THREE

LLEYTON immediately dived in after her as shock caused her to flail about helplessly.

But when he took her in a lifesaver's grip she started to splutter a protest. 'It's OK, I can swim—'

'It's not OK, you bloody idiot,' he ground out. 'The current is especially swift at half-tide. Just shut up and do as you're told.'

And, further to her ignominy, when he did manage to tow her to the bank downstream from the jetty there was a crowd gathered, and Ralph had even leapt onto the jet-ski and come zooming round.

Many hands helped them to crawl up to the grass, where they both lay winded and exhausted. Many voices expressed concern, but in the curiously restrained way people use when they're trying desperately not to laugh.

Nor were things helped when Lleyton sat up, obviously still in the grip of sheer rage, and said savagely, 'You're a walking bloody disaster, Vivian Florey! How the hell can one twenty-five-year-old slip of a girl get herself into so much trouble?'

Once again deathly silence reigned. Then Vivian sat up, coughed, dragged her hair out of her eyes, looked down the sopping, muddy and torn length of her to her once beautiful but now squelching Italian boots, and said, 'The trouble with you, Lleyton Dexter, is that you're too darn full of yourself and you've got no sense of humour!' And she put her head in her hands and started to laugh and hiccup until she was almost crying.

* * *

At six o'clock that evening there was a tap on her bedroom door.

The bedroom she'd been allotted looked out over the river, over which the sun had just set, and was spacious, decorated in lilac and hyacinth-blue and had its own bathroom. It opened out onto the upstairs verandah and the scent of jasmine was wafting in.

She'd just taken another shower, having slept dreamlessly for a couple of hours since her first shower, after being manhandled from the Hawkesbury.

Amelia Dexter had come to her rescue and smoothly contrived, after those moments of utter farce on the bank, to separate Vivian from Lleyton. She'd done more; she'd contrived to take Vivian under her wing and even make her feel like the victim of an unfortunate accident rather than a "bloody idiot".

She'd insisted on helping her to struggle out of her clothes in a downstairs bathroom, brought her a robe after her shower and ushered her up to this bedroom, where her bag had already been unpacked; she had also insisted, with what had appeared to be genuine concern, that she have a rest. She'd even managed to make Vivian feel like a cherished and cosseted guest and had told her where her own bedroom was—in case, she'd said, she needed anything.

So now, although she was wearing only a lilac seersucker robe over her underwear and had her head wrapped in a matching towel, both of which had come with the *en suite* bathroom, Vivian assumed it was Amelia knocking at her door and went to open it immediately.

It was Lleyton. Wearing a pair of charcoal trousers, a pale grey shirt open at the neck and a grey sports jacket with thin charcoal lines. He had two glasses in his hands.

'Oh, it's you,' she said unenthusiastically, then took a

deep breath and launched into her pre-planned speech, 'Look, I'm awfully sorry for what I did. It was extremely foolish of me and I didn't even have the decency to thank you for saving my life—'

'Forget it, Vivian,' he said abruptly. 'Can I come in? I've brought us a brandy each.'

She studied him for a moment but couldn't for the life of her decipher his expression. She retreated reluctantly, then closed the door behind him.

There were two wicker basket chairs beside a round table in one corner of the room and he put the drinks down on it.

'Is that—' she gestured to the crystal tumblers with their amber contents '—to be my last drink before I'm taken out and shot?'

He said nothing for a long moment, and there was a stillness about him as his gaze drifted over her that made her feel oddly tense because it seemed to say Beware—danger. The kind of danger she'd already identified in relation to Lleyton Dexter; the sort of thing that always seemed to strip any encounter between them down to a physical confrontation. An awareness of each other despite their hostility or, perhaps even heightened because of it.

She knew she could certainly be angry with him—she was right now—but that didn't alter her perception of the other criteria that shaped their dealings with each other. This awareness told her she couldn't remain unmoved when he undressed her mentally, and more so now, having experienced the feel of his hands on her, having been kissed and physically aroused by him.

But that was different, she told herself with some confusion as her nerves started to tingle and her senses came alive under his intent dark blue scrutiny. That wasn't a contest. That was, despite her denial, a reaction to him alone, but to the other side of Lleyton Dexter. To the man who had given her confidence and treated her like an equal, a man who was obviously capable and unafraid, even hero material, and wildly attractive to her.

Yet nothing physical had changed. He was still hero material—from his dark-fair hair, the lines of his face she was coming to know so well and the width of his shoulders to the easy strength of his body. So it was this mood that frightened her, this implication that there was only one place for them to go, and that was to bed…

'What do you mean?' he said at length.

'I…well, I gather we've come to the parting of the ways.' She paused and modulated her voice, which seemed to have got a bit high-pitched. 'Not that I could blame you. It's obvious that we can't go on after—well, what happened, and I won't even blame you for taking Clover Wines with you—'

'That's very noble of you, Vivian,' he said dryly, 'but it wasn't my intention.'

'I…you…you did say forget it when I started to apologise,' she stammered.

'How long have you been rehearsing that stilted little speech?' he asked with a ghost of a smile.

She flinched visibly, then decided to soldier on. 'Anyway, I sort of assumed that I would be flown out of Harvest Moon at first light—although you could send me to the nearest station and I could make my own way home. I'd prefer that, actually.'

'After being so brave on the plane?'

She shrugged and sat down. He put a glass in her hands and sat down opposite.

'Besides which—' his lips twisted '—you're the toast of the place. With most people,' he amended.

Vivian blinked, then put her glass down untasted to unwind the towel from her hair and run her fingers through it. 'Because,' she said cautiously, 'I...?'

His gaze rested on the riot of damp curls. 'Because you told me where to get off? Yes. But also because they feel a bit guilty.'

'What on earth for?' She reached for the brandy and took a sip.

'Vivian.' He sat forward and rolled his glass in his hands, 'Because Ginny and I have been divorced for over three years. Because she shouldn't be here. I didn't know she was—it was a misguided plot, hatched between my mother, my sister and Marlene. And why I have to be saddled with a godmother who'd make a good witch I have no idea,' he said bitterly, 'but it was a plot to bring us back together again.'

'All the same,' Vivian said slowly, 'would Virginia have gone along with it unless she wanted a chance to mend things?'

'There's no chance of that. It's over,' he said flatly.

'That's not quite the same thing, Lleyton. I mean, could your pride be involved, for example? Especially if she gave you your marching orders?'

He swore, then said wearily, 'Don't you start, Vivian. You have no idea...' He stopped and sat back, swallowed some brandy.

Vivian sipped her own drink and drew the hyacinth seersucker across her knees more securely. 'You're right, of course. And I won't presume to offer advice on something I know so little about—'

'Most obliging of you.'

She shot him a fiery little glance. 'Yes. Well, I still can't help wondering whether—even if you didn't know your ex-wife was going to be here—it doesn't have something to do with your bribing *me* to be here as a protection against your family—who are obviously a little mad—rather than simply being a buffer zone from predatory women at large, which is not quite the same thing!'

'You're right. I felt quite sure they'd have *someone* lined up for me, but I underestimated them.'

Vivian put her glass down on the table between them with something of a snap, but managed to stem the hot words that rose—only just.

He raised an eyebrow. 'But then I never hid from you the other reason I asked you to pose as my fiancée.'

She looked at him broodingly.

'You were the one,' he went on softly, but with a lethal kind of satire, 'who decided to try to ignore the sparks between us and who, right at this moment, is annoyed to think you're only here as my buffer zone.'

Was she? she wondered wildly, even as she moved restlessly beneath his gaze then got up and walked to the French door to evade it. 'If you think that makes you more legitimate than it makes me, Lleyton,' she said, 'may I make an observation? When you look at me as a possible candidate for your harem, it tends to bring out the worst in me,' she finished through her teeth.

'When did I do that?'

She turned back to him. 'You do it all the time. You even admit it!'

'I've never had a harem, never intend to,' he drawled. 'But I can't deny it's crossed my mind to wonder what we'd be like in bed. Are you saying it hasn't crossed yours?'

Vivian looked away and tried to force herself to relax, but there was tension stamped into every line of her figure as she did battle with honesty, pride and a feeling of sheer wariness again.

'Because if it hasn't,' he said idly, 'despite the context, I would say it's rather unusual to go around kissing men the way you kissed me, let alone agreeing to this in the first place.' He raised an eyebrow at her. 'Wouldn't you?'

Her throat worked but nothing came out, and she clenched her hands into fists.

He waited, watching her carefully for a long moment, then, 'Why would it be so hard to admit it, Vivian?'

'Because I don't choose to,' she said flatly, at last released from speechlessness.

'Yet, talking of context, we stimulate each other in a very physical way, as well as mentally.' He paused and glanced over towards the queen-size bed. 'Personally—' a faint smile twisted his lips '—I think it wouldn't only be a celebration of your courage but your body and your feisty spirit that would be worthy of the finest wine—a celebration of life and the attraction between two people of like mind.'

Vivian closed her eyes briefly and thought that she'd never be able to lie in that bed without seeing the images he'd aroused, of them making love... She clenched her teeth and forced her mind away from it at the same time as she acknowledged she'd underestimated Lleyton Dexter, and certainly overestimated her ability to be indifferent to him.

Then he drained his glass and stood up. 'So, on that basis alone, Vivian, I don't see why we shouldn't continue what we started. Do you?'

There was a couple of feet of lilac carpet separating them and it seemed vitally important to her to achieve some kind of detachment from this man and the effect he had on her. But, as his gaze roamed over her, she was all too aware of the disadvantage of being caught in her underwear and robe. And it wasn't only that. It was how she was starting to be affected by the little things about him.

It was not just the aura of a devastatingly attractive and powerful man now. There was the way one eyebrow quirked when he was genuinely amused, the way the watch on his lean wrist looked so essentially masculine to her. There were his hands, long and strong—she had several bruises from being rescued by him from the river to prove how strong, and yet when he'd kissed her they'd slid over the skin of her throat with the lightest touch. And, having once felt that, how did you banish the tendency to wonder how would it feel to have those hands stroke your breasts?

She felt the colour start to rise from the base of her throat and put her own hand up to close her robe at the neck.

He followed the movement with his eyes, then they narrowed on her upper arm, where the short sleeve of the robe had slipped back.

'Did I do that?' he asked with a frown.

'What?'

He crossed the carpet and put his fingertips on her skin, about halfway between her elbow and shoulder. 'This bruise?'

'Oh.' She looked down at it. 'Yes, plus a couple more, but I'd rather have a few bruises than be found floating face-down in the river,' she managed to say lightly.

'All the same I'm sorry.'

'That's OK.'

'Because you have skin like silk, Vivian,' he said very quietly, and ran his fingers down her arm, 'and a lovely figure. You also kissed me rather uniquely.'

How? She didn't say it, but for a moment her eyes were wide with the question, and she wasn't helped when he lifted his fingers to touch her mouth, then pushed both of his hands into his pockets.

He said, quite soberly, 'I can't help wondering if some man didn't leave you a bit bruised mentally.'

She swallowed, and said gruffly, 'Because I haven't rushed into your arms, Lleyton?'

'Because you've come into them when you couldn't help yourself but don't care to admit it,' he observed.

She couldn't say anything. It was if they were caught in a net of memories of the airstrip, as if that blue gaze travelling down her slim outline in the lilac seersucker had the power to take her back as well as make her feel as if her body was on display for Lleyton Dexter. And not only that, but also her mind, although he said nothing more, did nothing. But he didn't have to, of course. She now knew only too well the kind of rapture he could dispense, and that his mere presence was enough to remind her of it.

'Look,' she said awkwardly, desperate to end the sheer intimacy of the moment, then bit her lip and sighed as she saw her dilemma all too clearly. If she told him that Goodman & Associates had its back to the wall at the moment, and that was why she was doing this, might she not give him cause to doubt the wisdom of putting any accounts in their way? On the other hand, especially now, she needed a reason for being here...

'Look,' she said again, 'it was never part of *my* plan to have to sleep with you to get the Clover shampoo account, or the wines, but it is important to the agency—'

'Forget the shampoo,' he murmured, looking down at her quizzically now. 'You've got it anyway.'

'What's more,' she continued, in what she hoped would be a cool, logical demolition of Lleyton Dexter, and then suddenly realised what he'd said. *'What?'*

'You've got it, Vivian,' he said deliberately. 'Julianna Jones can rest easy and you don't have to change a hair of her head.'

'You mean I can't lose it even if I...refuse ever to have anything to do with you?'

'Precisely. Uh—I'll leave you to get dressed. Dinner will be ready in half an hour.'

Vivian gestured dazedly. 'What about the wine account?'

'Ah.' He paused. 'That may take a little longer.'

'And you talk about being legitimate,' she marvelled bitterly. 'So I've got to carry on with this impossible charade to get it? I can't do it,' she said flatly. 'I would never have agreed to it in the first place if I'd known about your ex-wife. Yes, OK, it is important to Goodmans, but I've said it before and I'll say it again—a faceless bunch of women is a different thing from an ex-wife!'

'I'm sure she'd agree,' he said wryly. 'By the way, she's decided to stay on. She is a very good friend of Mag's. And I thought we'd established at least one other good reason for you to stay—only a few moments ago as well as this morning,' he murmured.

This silenced Vivian quite effectively. So much so that he laughed softly and moved a step forward to touch her cheek, which was flaming again, with the tips of his fingers. 'Why don't you just stay on as yourself? Everyone has a fair idea that you and I are not exactly a couple made in heaven, anyway.'

He walked out.

Vivian sat down and finished her drink in one gulp. But the furious thought plus the burst of warmth that slid through her veins from the brandy produced only one conclusion. For tonight, at least, she had no option but to stay.

And half an hour later Amelia came to get her.

* * *

'Very nice,' she said approvingly of Vivian's terracotta crêpe mini dress that clung to her figure, was sleeveless and had a low square neck—but she wore it with a pale filmy open blouse to hide the bruises on her arm. With it she wore a pair of mules with closed toes and little heels that matched her dress.

Amelia was clad in a flowing colourful silk caftan.

'How do you feel now, my dear?' she added. 'Lleyton assures me he's smoothed things over.'

Vivian raised an eyebrow. 'What Lleyton may think of as smoothing things over is actually more like steamrollering— Uh, I'm sorry, Mrs Dexter, I shouldn't have said that. I have a slightly unguarded tongue.'

'Which I find very refreshing, Vivian. Please don't feel you have to guard it on my account.'

'Well…' Vivian shrugged. 'I may not be able to—but he is your son.'

'That doesn't mean to say I approve of Lleyton getting his own way over everything! Shall we go down? We're having a buffet supper tonight.'

'It so happens I'm starving, Mrs Dexter. I could eat a horse—must be something to do with getting all but drowned,' she said with a grin.

Amelia Dexter, who had dark blue eyes just like her son, gazed at Vivian thoughtfully for a moment. Then she said straightly, 'I don't approve of divorce, Vivian, I have to confess. So I've lived in hope that Lleyton and Ginny could patch up their differences. I still do. But in different circumstances I feel I would have liked you, my dear.' She put her arm through Vivian's, as if to take the sting out of it, and added, 'By the way, please call me Amelia. I may be quite old, but nothing makes me feel older than "Mrs Dexter"!'

* * *

The buffet was served in a glassed-in conservatory at the back of the house. Instead of one large table there were several smaller round ones and no prearranged seating plan. You took pot luck.

Not that that could used as a way of describing the food, despite it being a buffet. There was vichyssoise, or melon with smoked salmon in mayonnaise with capers, chopped olives and capsicum as an entrée. There was cold ham carved from the bone with a variety of salads to choose from, or a sweet and sour pork dish and rice for the main course, and three magnificent pavlovas with strawberries, kiwi fruit, bananas and passion fruit together with ice cream for dessert.

And the ambience, Vivian decided, was fantastic. Candlelight, wrought-iron tables and chairs, big pottery tubs of orange and mandarin trees dotted about, casting mysterious shadows like the delicate brushstrokes of an oriental artist on the glass.

It also came to mind that a considerable fortune would be required to keep Harvest Moon alone going. A thought that made her pause during her sweet and sour pork and look penetratingly at Lleyton, whom she'd contrived to ignore until now, seated beside her.

'Have I done something wrong?' he asked after a moment.

'Not at all. I was just thinking how very rich you must be.'

His lips twisted. 'No comment,' he murmured, glancing at his watch, and he stood up. 'Would you excuse me? I've got an important call coming in from Singapore. I won't be long.'

'Sure,' she said blithely.

'One would have imagined you already knew how rich

he was, Vivian,' Marlene Wainright said as her godson passed out of earshot. She was seated opposite, with Ralph between her and Vivian and Eddie between her and Lleyton's place.

Although inwardly cursing herself for making what had been meant as an idle comment audible to others, Vivian said lightly, 'It's nothing I hold against him. Not that much anyway.'

'We didn't think you'd be complaining, dear.'

Both Ralph and Eddie moved restlessly as Vivian put her knife and fork down and stared at the woman opposite. Marlene Wainright was in her sixties, she judged, but, unlike her bosom pal, Amelia Dexter, used no artifice to disguise her age. In fact she reminded Vivian of a rather scrawny, silver-headed eagle with her piercing yet heavy-lidded eyes.

'Well, let's not pussyfoot around, Lady Wainright,' she said evenly. 'Am I a gold-digging fortune-huntress? Of course I am. And poor Lleyton knows it but he just can't help himself. Still, I keep telling myself he's free and thirty-five, and he really should know how to look after himself by now, don't you think?' she finished with gentle irony.

Marlene Wainright sucked in a furious breath, then picked up her plate and left the table in a high dudgeon.

'Oh, my stars,' Ralph breathed, and buried his face behind his napkin to hide his helpless laughter, 'Vivian, where have you been for most of my life?'

Eddie, also struggling with mirth, choked on his wine and said unsteadily, 'Not to mention mine and Mag's!'

But Vivian had come tumbling down to earth. 'Why on earth did I do that?' She closed her eyes.

'Don't regret it,' Ralph advised. 'It's about time someone gave the old bat her comeuppance.'

'But I do regret it,' Vivian assured him, and turned to Eddie. 'I seem to be destined to throw your wedding week into turmoil. I'm almost tempted to think Lleyton's right—I am a walking disaster.'

'I'm sure Lleyton didn't mean that,' Eddie said comfortingly. 'Just heat of the moment, you know. And it would be a miracle if we got to the altar without a few disasters.'

'I'm exhausted,' Vivian said to Lleyton at about eleven o'clock.

They were alone on the terrace after an evening of cards and other games like carpet bowls.

'It was all rather lively,' he commented.

'No, it was fun, that part of it. I'm exhausted from guarding my tongue and trying to work out who genuinely likes me and at least one person who genuinely hates me.'

'Who would that be?'

'Your godmother,' Vivian said bleakly. 'We—clashed while you were away talking to Singapore.' She told him what had been said, adding, 'I can't understand why your mother, who seems to be rather nice, has a friend like that.'

'They were at school together. Marlene lost her son, her only child, in an accident when he was fifteen. She's never really got over it. Then she lost her husband. That's why my mother keeps an eye on her.'

'Now I feel really terrible,' Vivian said after a short silence. They were sitting on a teak bench and, although she couldn't see the river, she fancied there was a light mist rising from it, and the night was full of scents to her keen nose. From the bushland, the water and the garden.

Lleyton shrugged. 'She always was a rather acid kind

of person, but it's intensified. And from what you've told me, she fired the first shot.'

'She did, but—oh, what the hell! Where is everyone?' Vivian asked. 'I had no intention of being private with you again this evening, incidentally,' she added gloomily.

He stretched his arms along the back of the bench and looked down at her wryly. 'Here and there. Going to bed, most of them. Diplomatically giving us the opportunity to be alone, the rest of them. I would say Ralph and Eddie don't have the slightest problem with you, Vivian.'

She blinked. 'Perhaps not, but they're men.'

'One of whom is my brother, the other about to marry my sister.'

'Oh, I don't mean like that! Well, perhaps a bit in Ralph's case,' she amended. 'Although men do see women through different eyes, don't they?' She sat upright suddenly. 'You're not warning me off either of them by any chance, are you?' she asked ominously.

'I'm just saying that how you interact with other men could have a bearing on how some of the women in this…circus might view you.'

'I've only just met them,' she protested incredulously. 'I haven't had a chance to interact with anyone—this is ridiculous and doesn't become you, Lleyton Dexter!'

He smiled slightly. 'You played a mean and lively game of boule with Ralph as your partner. You did also give me to understand you found his type of man quite thrilling.'

'Only to take you down a peg or two!'

'Really?'

'Yes, really. What is this anyway? Are *you* now wondering whether I'm a fortune-huntress?' She stared at him under the dim terrace lamp with the light of battle in her eyes. 'It's not *you* or your brother I want, don't forget.'

He picked up her hand and looked at it. 'So you say, but we'll leave that for the moment. No, I was just warning you, Vivian.' He slid her slender fingers through his. 'Ralph can be funny, good company and all the rest, but he has one singular failure. He has always resented me and done his best to throw a spanner in the works—especially when it comes to women.'

Vivian's lips parted. 'Oh, no…not with Ginny?' she whispered.

'No. He wouldn't still be here if he had,' Lleyton said coolly, so coolly Vivian shivered. 'But you could be a different matter.'

'Because he's sensed I'm not for real?' she suggested tartly.

'Something like that,' Lleyton agreed smoothly.

'Glory be,' she said with difficulty, 'what on earth have I got myself into?'

'A family—something you may not know much about, I believe. They can be absolute cauldrons of emotion at the best of times—when you have the added complications we have, they can be sheer hell.'

'How did you know that?' She frowned at him. 'That I have no family?'

He moved his shoulders. 'Your boss, Stan Goodman.'

'You've been checking up on me?'

'Not at all. No, he rang me, as a matter of fact. And issued a rather pointed little warning.'

'Stan did that?' she said softly, and all of a sudden discovered that she had tears on her lashes.

He glanced at her, released her hand and put his arm around her shoulders. 'Don't be sad.'

'I can't help it; I don't know why. I mean, I don't know why *now*, of all times. I guess I'll always miss my father, but…' She shrugged and leant her head on his shoulder.

'It's been a big day,' he suggested. 'Enough to make anyone emotional. Flying, a forced swim and confronting a whole heap of strangers, some of whom have looked at you with deep suspicion.'

'Mmm,' she agreed. 'Your sister for one. She and your ex-wife delicately avoided me all evening.'

'That bothers you?' he asked quietly.

Vivian tilted her chin and smiled up at him. 'I know it shouldn't in view of my sentiments on the subject of yourself, Lleyton, but they both seem rather nice. So, yes. But—' she yawned suddenly '—I don't think it's going to affect my sleep.'

'That's good to hear.'

'The only problem is I don't seem to have the will or the energy to go anywhere at the moment.'

He laughed softly and kissed the top of her head. 'I could always be very manly and carry you up to bed.'

'Were we going to the same bed, Lleyton, I might accept, and I think that's what you should reserve that kind of gesture for,' she responded. 'And even then, speaking as unbiased observer, don't you think it might be taxing most men's manliness to have to climb a set of stairs like these at Harvest Moon carrying a girl before—well, you know what? A few steps over a threshold is a different matter…' She stopped and started to chuckle.

'Vivian, if nothing else, getting to know you has been a salutary lesson. However, I should issue a warning. Whilst I won't go out of my way to prove you wrong about the stairs, I might be tempted to prove you wrong on the kissing issue. Again.'

'You shouldn't,' she said slowly. 'I was feeling rather comforted and safe. You know…' She frowned. 'It's as if you're two people. The man who got me to fly with him, for example, and the…match that's going to burn my fingers.' Her tone was suddenly dry.

'As an admission of anything, Vivian, that was—well, I guess it was a start,' he said with a faint smile.

She sat up, although still within the circle of his arm, and looked into his eyes. 'There's no future for us in that direction at the moment. There's nothing *real* between us, Lleyton.'

'No? Oh, well, at least you qualified it to "at the moment".' He smiled wryly. 'Small mercies, maybe only crumbs from the table, but that kind of thing.'

She frowned again. 'You are a strange man.'

'How so?'

'Well, sometimes you're fairly ordinary, sometimes you're very much the tycoon, but right now you're…humble, and it's almost as if this isn't a *deal*.'

He raised an eyebrow but said nothing.

'Then again, could it be a game?' she said slowly, as if thinking aloud.

'Tell you what,' he offered, 'why don't you sleep on it and let me know your considered opinion in the morning?'

She stood up and stared down at him almost sombrely. Then she said goodnight abruptly and disappeared indoors.

Leaving Lleyton Dexter to ponder what exactly he did have in mind for Vivian Florey, and what he should expect her to come up with in the morning.

It was Ralph who broke into his reflections. He appeared around the corner of the verandah like a dark shadow and sat down on the bench.

'You don't know her from a bar of soap, do you, Lleyton?'

'I might have known someone would be listening in,' Lleyton said dryly. 'And that it would most likely be you.'

'I don't know what I missed. I'd only been there a moment or two, but long enough to hear about the ''deal'' bit,' Ralph replied. 'Why, though?'

'Why what?'

'Did you have to *rent* a girl?' Ralph said deliberately. 'I'd love to know what kind of deal was involved. Money? Job? And don't think I'm the only one speculating, pal,' he added with irony. 'Mag's of the same opinion. So is—'

'Excuse me!'

They both turned to see Vivian standing a few paces away, looking flustered and as if she'd just run down the stairs.

Lleyton stood up. 'What's wrong?'

'My ring,' she said tragically, 'I can't find it. Oh, please tell me I gave it to you to look after and it's not sitting at the bottom of the river.'

Lleyton opened his mouth, closed it and said in a slightly unsteady way, 'I've got it. But if you promise not to fall into the river again, you'll be quite safe wearing it here.'

'Oh, thank heavens,' Vivian breathed, and, clutching his lapels, she stood on tiptoe and kissed him. 'Can I have it now, darling? I do promise I won't do anything silly, because I really treasure it.'

'Why not?' he murmured. 'Let's go and get it.'

He took her to a study on the ground floor and opened a safe behind a large picture after firmly closing the French windows and drawing the curtains. 'You heard, I gather?' he said ruefully.

'I heard,' she repeated furiously. 'And if anyone thinks

I'm going to stay around as a rent-a-girl, they're much mistaken!'

Lleyton found the grey velvet box and closed the safe. 'How did you come to hear?'

Vivian eyed him haughtily. 'I turned back to tell you that I really did appreciate all you'd done one way and another today. I'm not ungrateful,' she said stiffly.

He opened the box and put it on the desk. Then he looked at her meditatively. There were shadows of tiredness beneath her eyes but defiance and spirit stamped into every line of her figure. 'That was worthy of an Oscar, Vivian.'

'It's amazing what you can do when people are taking a hammer to your reputation,' she retorted.

'So I see, but this—' he plucked the ring out of the box '—is perpetuating the charade. Something you were dead keen not to do earlier,' he reminded her.

'I've changed my mind.' She put out her hand, palm up, for the ring. 'I didn't think you'd object.'

He didn't hand the ring over, but stood twisting it around thoughtfully. 'I'm just issuing a warning, I guess,' he said with a faint smile. 'When you've cooled down you may regret this.'

'No, I won't.' She tossed her head. 'OK, I was mad ever to agree to this, but now I've got myself into it I might as well go the whole hog. Don't argue with me, Lleyton, I'm tired!' she added.

His lips twisted. 'Don't say I didn't warn you, Vivian. Which hand, left or right?'

'Left.' She turned her hand over. 'Just don't get carried away or go down on your bended knee,' she said with a sudden spark of mischief.

He slid the ring on without bending his knees—he took her in his arms instead.

'Lleyton,' she protested.

'Vivian?'

There was a glint of mockery in his eyes as their gazes clashed, then his gaze slid to the low square neck of her dress and his hands came up to slide the blouse away so he could cup the curves of her shoulders. 'Perhaps I should take you flying more often,' he said softly.

'I don't think that would be a very good idea.'

His eyebrow quirked. 'You might get too used to it and not be prompted to kiss me so…wholeheartedly?' He took his hands from her shoulders, but only to slip them around her waist.

'Yes,' she agreed with an effort. 'No… I mean…' She trailed off frustratedly, because she didn't know what she meant at all. It was extremely difficult to concentrate, in fact.

'Tell me about all these men you've liked a lot more than me but hated kissing?'

She bit her lip. 'That wasn't entirely true. I mean, there haven't been *lots* of them—'

'That is what you gave me to understand,' he pointed out lazily.

Vivian took a little breath and wrenched her mind from the sensation of his hands resting on her hips, a sensation that was extremely nerve-racking because it was quite lovely but likely to lead her along the path of no redemption, she feared. 'Um…OK, if you really want to know. It was true. I didn't like being kissed. I never thought I would. Other things—' she shrugged '—were all right.'

'Only all right?' he murmured wickedly.

She frowned as Ryan Dempsey swam into her mind's eye—as it happened the only point of reference she had on which to base a comparison to how Lleyton Dexter made her feel. And her lips parted and her eyebrows rose suddenly, because it had taken Ryan six months to get her to agree that she wanted him as much as he wanted her, and she still hadn't been sure that the mental and companionship side of their relationship had meant more to her, anyway. Whereas it had taken Lleyton four days to…

He broke into her reverie. 'Am I being compared to some former lover, Vivian?'

Her eyes widened, her cheeks went pink and she moved, embarrassed. But she couldn't find a thing to say.

'Going to tell me how I've scored so far?'

That did elicit a response. 'Definitely not,' she said frostily.

'So you're not the kind of girl to sleep and tell?'

'I don't know what makes you think you have the right to do this, Lleyton, but I think it's…gratuitous!' She brought out the word triumphantly.

He laughed and kissed her forehead. 'You are wearing my engagement ring, Vivian.'

'And you promised me a straight and honourable deal!'

'I have yet to seduce you, my dear,' he said, still looking amused. 'Also, much as I hate to repeat myself—'

'I started it,' she broke in, and sighed heavily. 'OK. I stand convicted.'

'You didn't start it—it happened,' he said quietly. 'But you didn't exactly repel it either.'

'I know.' She sighed again, and looked up into his eyes honestly. 'But I'm still afraid of getting my fingers burnt,' she warned soberly. 'And for the duration of this deal,' she added stubbornly, 'I'm not going to let it get into anything more.'

'OK,' he said casually, but picked her up and took her over to the buttoned leather settee.

'I don't…' She started to say, trying to get up but being restrained from doing so.

'Relax, Vivian,' he ordered, and waited a moment before adding, 'Comfortable?'

'I don't seem to have much choice.' She'd ended up sitting beside him with his arm around her.

'No, you don't. At the moment,' he said with a wicked little glint. 'Because we need to get some things sorted out.'

Vivian sighed, squirmed a bit to make herself more comfortable, and the pressure of his arm relaxed. She also kicked off her shoes and tucked her feet up beside her on the settee. 'What?'

'Are you resisting "us" because of business or because you're afraid of getting involved with a man?'

Vivian studied the ring on her left hand, spreading her fingers, then forming a fist. 'A bit of both.' She looked up into his eyes at last. 'Don't think I don't know I should never have agreed to this in the first place, but you did...' She stopped frustratedly.

'Throw down the kind of gauntlet you couldn't refuse?' he suggested.

'Exactly. I really should have stuck to my first idea on how to impress a girl other than bribing her.'

'Why don't you let me have a go at that?'

This time it was a considering glance with which she favoured him. 'As in kissing me whenever the whim takes you?'

'Not necessarily. But being together in accord for a start.'

Vivian looked down at the ring again, and a thought struck her. '*Did* you buy this for me, Lleyton?'

'Yes.'

She sat up as if she'd been shot.

'But it was a good investment at the same time.'

She subsided. 'I might have known! Oh, well, you win

some and lose some.' She grinned. 'For a moment I quite thought I had made a really deep impression on you, Lleyton Dexter, which was slightly electrifying. Quite a heady sense of power, actually. But I'm back with my feet on the ground and I'm going to bed.'

'You haven't responded,' he pointed out. 'In fact you would appear to be ducking the issue.'

She bit her lip. 'I...I don't know,' she said slowly. 'I...'

'Tell me one thing before you go to bed, Vivian. We are after all sitting together almost as lovers would.'

She stirred, realised she had her head on his shoulder again with his arms still tucked about her waist, and grimaced. 'What?'

'Who was he?'

'Someone I worked with, that's all.'

'And you thought you loved him?' he queried.

She was silent for a while. 'I thought so, yes. I thought it was mutual but I was wrong,' she said eventually. 'Of course I could have been the unsatisfactory factor, easily. How about you?'

He disengaged his arm and stood up. Vivian waited for a moment, then stood up herself. 'You must have been in love with Ginny to marry her,' she heard herself say, although some form of mental warning bell was going off in her head. A bell that seemed to tell her she shouldn't be admitting this kind of interest in Lleyton and his relationship with Ginny Deacon. But it was, at the same time, something she couldn't help herself from wanting to know.

They were standing face to face about a foot apart, so her face was tilted up to him.

He raised a hand as if to touch her cheek, then paused,

and dropped it. 'Yes. So I thought, at least. It died a natural death when I found out she was in fact selling herself to me, and that she'd deliberately got herself pregnant to…cement the deal.'

CHAPTER FOUR

VIVIAN sat bolt upright in bed early the next morning, then lay back with a sigh as she held her left hand up and the pink diamond glittered on her finger.

She was still at Harvest Moon. She was in the luxurious bedroom with its lilac carpet, its hyacinth curtains that brushed the floor and were looped back around big brass knobs because she'd forgotten to close them last night. She was in the big bed with its hyacinth and white floral padded headboard that matched the quilted coverlet and pillow cases, lying between crisp white sheets.

She hadn't been mysteriously transported back to her own safe world on the wings of a dove—her lips curved into a smile that faded almost immediately. Because there was no doubt in her mind that she was walking a minefield. And not only the Dexter family's but her own.

She hadn't stayed to ask Lleyton for any more details, or to answer the questions that were burning in her brain—why had Ginny Deacon sold herself to Lleyton Dexter? And what had happened to the child? She'd rather fled, in fact, with a mumbled goodnight, and it had only been when she'd got to her room that she'd realised she'd left her shoes behind—she hadn't gone back to retrieve them.

But of course all this merely postponed thinking about the effect Lleyton Dexter had on one Vivian Florey, spinster, masquerading as his fiancée.

It wasn't cold, but she pulled the sheet and coverlet around her as a little shiver ran through her. Because yesterday, after knowing each other for a bare three days, he'd contrived to kiss her in a way that had been astonishingly…what?

'Riveting,' she supplied flatly to herself.

And she could no longer deny that she was finding Lleyton more and more dangerously attractive. Even to the point— No, surely not, she told herself. But honesty compelled her to admit it. To take up his suggestion that they get to know each other in accord rather than in this crazy scenario would be…OK. She flinched as she thought it, but the fact was, he'd achieved some minor miracles for her.

He'd actually got her to fly in a light plane with him. And he'd managed to make her feel celebrated and brave instead of an utter idiot. Of course he'd tarnished that reputation somewhat by calling her a walking disaster later, but that had been her own fault. He'd also saved her, in the process, from possible drowning. And he'd given her Clover Shampoo, although not the wine…

It was like a seesaw, she thought with a tinge of despair. How could you feel safe and comfortable at times with a man, then electrified and a bit terrified at the power he had to make you feel that way—and at others gloriously right in his arms? A man, she reminded herself, who'd got her into this in the first place by devious means. A man whose intentions were not at all clear to her. And now this. An ex-wife, a child…

Someone knocked on the door.

'Who is it?' she called cautiously.

'Breakfast, ma'am,' a girlish voice answered cheerfully.

'Come in!' Vivian sat up as a girl of about eighteen in a pink and white striped overall wheeled in a trolley. 'I didn't expect this.'

'Mrs Dexter,' the girl replied with a twinkle. 'She likes

to get people up and about. And she's got a boating expedition planned for today, so she's asked me to tell you she'd like everyone assembled on the jetty at ten o'clock. They're going to cruise upriver to a nice restaurant for lunch, then, when you get back, there's to be a croquet competition. Would you like tea or coffee, ma'am?'

'Coffee—sounds like some fancy resort,' Vivian commented, 'but this breakfast looks wonderful. Thank you so much—Belinda.' The girl had a name tag on her overall.

It did look wonderful: fruit and muesli, a herb omelette, toast and jam, cheese and fruit juice.

'Bon appétit,' Belinda said pertly, and left Vivian to it.

At a quarter to ten, Vivian strolled onto to the jetty.

She had in fact been down and about for quite a bit longer, walking to the airstrip and back. A good walk always did wonders for her, and although it hadn't produced any burst of inspiration on her personal problems she felt better—not quite sure how she was going to face Lleyton Dexter after running out on him the previous evening, but better in the sense that striding out along the airstrip road had given her the confidence that *she* was in charge of her destiny.

And she looked suitably nautical, she hoped, in white shorts and sand shoes, her white blouse with shells on it and a hot pink peaked cap that matched her raffia holdall. She wore a lemon bikini under her clothes and dark glasses completed the outfit. Sunscreen, a change of clothes, a towel—just in case she fell in again—and a light sweater were in the holdall which she'd left on the jetty.

Of course, the ring on her left hand could also be considered part of the outfit, she'd mused as she'd dressed, if not the most striking part of it. Why on earth hadn't she stopped to think last night?

She'd met no one on her walk, for which she'd been duly grateful, and she was the first to arrive for the cruise apart from Lleyton, who was already aboard, fiddling with the two powerful outboards that ran the boat. It was a magnificent day, sunny, cloudless and hot.

Just her luck, she thought ruefully, as she watched him unseen for a moment. Still, better to meet him without an audience, perhaps.

'Morning,' she said, perhaps a shade cautiously.

He lifted his head, squinted, and rubbed the back of his hand across his cheek, thereby transferring a streak of grease onto it. 'If it isn't Miss Florey, my reluctant fiancée,' he murmured, 'looking all bright and bushy-tailed.'

Vivian put her hands on her hips. 'Are you in a seriously bad mood with me, Mr Dexter?'

'Not at all,' he denied, but replaced the hood on one of the outboards with something of a thud.

'You do seem to be viewing the world through a jaundiced eye at the moment, or am I imagining it?'

'And you do seem to be balancing on the edge of the jetty again, Vivian,' he shot back.

She stepped off the coping hastily. 'Sorry. I... No, I won't say it.'

'Please don't hold back on my account,' he remarked bitterly, and replaced the second hood and climbed onto the jetty himself.

Vivian eyed him cautiously. In khaki trousers, a yellow T-shirt and brown leather deck shoes, his hair hanging in his eyes, he seemed to tower over her and was quite a sight, even with his distinctly moody expression.

'Well, I was only going to say that the only reason I

fell in yesterday was to do with getting a bit of a surprise. A big bit of a surprise.' She shrugged.

He folded his arms. 'As you did last night, I gather?'

'Yep. Life amongst the rich and famous is certainly a bit above the kind of thing I'm used to.'

'Rubbish,' he said. 'It happens to all manner of people.'

'Er—all manner of people are approaching, Lleyton,' she warned, looking past him. 'Your mother, your godmother, your sister, your ex-wife, Eddie, Ralph, the bridesmaids, your cousin Mary and—hallelujah! Some kids. I was beginning to wonder whether you kept them locked up in a zoo. But will we all fit into this boat?' She gestured towards the boat he'd been working on.

'All but two of us. You and I will be going in this one.' He gestured to a smaller speedboat, tied up on the other side of the jetty.

She opened her mouth but the crowd descended on them.

'If it isn't our two lovebirds!' Ralph said at large. 'Morning, Vivian. I see you haven't lost the ring yet. Do show us.'

What followed was more farce as Ralph possessed himself of her hand, whistled expressively, and offered it to Amelia Dexter for inspection.

'Very...nice,' Lleyton's mother said stiffly.

'Not only that,' Marlene Wainright remarked, peering over Amelia's shoulder, 'but quite expensive, I would imagine.'

'Sixty thousand dollars, I believe,' Vivian responded, and took her hand back serenely. 'I'm sure you're wondering if I'm worth it, but—'

'I'm quite sure you are, Vivian,' Lleyton intervened. 'OK, Ralph, you're skippering the main party; Vivian and I will ride gunshot. Let's get aboard.'

It took a good, noisy fifteen minutes to get everyone and their gear stowed on the bigger boat, during which Vivian sat on the coping, swinging her legs. There were four children, two girls and two boys, ranging from about three to ten, all pleasurably excited, although none of them seemed to be attached to either Lleyton or Ginny. In fact Ginny came and sat down next to Vivian during Operation Noah's Ark, as Lleyton called it. He had appeared to throw off his mood, and proved to be a dab hand with kids as he strapped them all into life jackets and passed them down the ladder to Ralph and Eddie.

She said, apparently sincerely, 'It's lovely.'

'It...oh, the ring. I guess it is.'

'You don't sound too sure,' Ginny said with a humorous glint in her striking, pale eyes. 'I wouldn't take too much notice of Lady Wainright. She can be a thorn in all our sides.'

Vivian glanced at her. Her straight, very fair hair was tied back beneath a blue linen sunhat and she wore denim shorts with a voluminous white linen blouse. She contrived to look essentially casual though marvellously chic and her figure—she was taller than Vivian—was slender and graceful.

'I...didn't know about you. I'm sorry,' Vivian said.

The other girl's carefully darkened brows rose. 'I thought not. Lleyton can be very selective about what he tells people.'

'You're not wrong,' Vivian said darkly. 'That's why I fell into the river yesterday. I had no idea he had an ex-wife. Can I ask you something?'

'Yes, although I may not be able to answer you,' Ginny Deacon said slowly.

'Do you love him—did you ever?'

'Oh, yes. But loving Lleyton is asking to get your heart

broken—well, I think all they need is me!' She stood up and nimbly climbed down the ladder.

Vivian stood up too, and she and Lleyton watched as Ralph carefully edged the boat out into the river, then gunned the motors. They waved back to most of the occupants.

'Ready?' he queried.

'As I ever will be.'

'You're not paranoid about boats, by any chance?'

'Not in the slightest,' she replied furiously, and without waiting for a hand climbed down into the smaller craft to sit in one of the two padded chairs.

He followed, but didn't start the motor immediately. 'I gather I've offended you?'

'Yes, you have. Not only that, you've disappointed me,' she retorted. 'Yesterday you were wonderful about my fear of flying. Today you've undone all that at a single stroke!' She folded her arms and stared after the bigger boat sternly.

He said, not quite smiling, 'I humbly beg your forgiveness, Vivian. To be in your bad books is quite terrifying.'

'Rubbish!' She turned to him, but as he started to laugh openly some of her ire left her; she wasn't sure why.

'I've never met anyone who packed quite the punch you do,' he said. 'I hope you never change. Ready now?'

She hesitated, then nodded.

He pulled on a peaked cap and sunglasses and started the motor. Moments later they were planing at some speed up the Hawkesbury. It was exhilarating.

'Ever water-skied?' he asked.

'No! But I'm sure it's fun.' She found she was starting to feel a lot better.

He slowed down and turned the boat so their wake was

a perfect silvery arc on the brown waters and nosed it into a lovely little crescent of beach rimmed by thick bush.

'I thought we were riding shotgun?' she said.

He pointed to a VHF radio on the dashboard. 'Ralph can get in touch with us if anything goes wrong, but he's no slouch with boats himself. You wouldn't have thought to bring a costume with you?'

'I happen to be wearing one—are we giving the rest of the party the slip, by any chance?' she asked slowly.

'They don't need us for the moment. There are enough of them, one would have thought.' He pressed a button and the anchor chain rattled out.

Vivian stood up and looked at the water longingly. Without the wind rushing past them it was seriously hot now. 'Just a couple of things. I could dive off this boat—is it deep enough?'

He nodded.

'What about the famous—or infamous tide?'

'It's about to turn; that's when a tide is at its slackest. You'll have no problem.'

'Oh. But how do I get back on?'

Lleyton rummaged through a locker and produced a rope ladder, which he hooked over the side. 'Like so.'

'I see you have every possibility taken care of—OK, here goes!' She unbuttoned her blouse, slipped her shoes, cap, and her shorts off and put her ring into its box, which she happened to have in her holdall, then, at a second thought apparently, she pulled a T-shirt out and put it on.

'Are you planning to swim or walk across the water?' Lleyton asked wryly as he began to strip off his clothes.

'Protect myself from the sun,' she answered blandly, and dived in.

As soon as she surfaced she set out at a fast crawl for

the beach. And although Lleyton was only moments behind her she beat him to it.

'Pretty impressive, Miss Florey,' he said as they stood up with water streaming off them.

Vivian wiped her hair out of her eyes and laughed at him. 'I'm so glad I'm impressive in some respect!'

His eyes narrowed thoughtfully, and although he said nothing she got the impression he had divined her intention to keep things as light as possible—an intention that had come upon her because she had no idea how else to proceed, she thought rather ruefully. But confronted by Lleyton Dexter in a pair of dark blue board shorts and nothing else to hide the width of his shoulders, his flat trim torso and long brown legs after he'd stripped off his T-shirt and trousers, some plan had to be devised.

'You're very impressive at your work,' he said then, and led the way to a flat rock with a natural basin in the middle full of water. He scooped the water over the surface so they could sit down without getting scalded.

'That's different,' she said humorously, 'although even there I can be a walking disaster.'

'Client relations?' he hazarded, looking down at her, not quite smiling again.

'As you've seen, I can put my foot in my mouth. This is heaven!' She stood up and waded into the water again, then came out and scooped some more water out of the basin and sank down beside him. 'By the look of that bush—' she gestured '—no one could get here by road certainly, and not even on foot.'

'It is a favourite little private spot of mine,' he agreed.

'Well, thanks for sharing it. Especially since I…may not be your favourite person at the moment.'

'Who said that?'

'You may not have said it but your attitude certainly implied it when we first met this morning.'

There was a short silence. 'I was feeling slightly jaundiced towards the world at large this morning,' he admitted finally, then shrugged. 'Or perhaps it was myself.'

Vivian shot him a glance from beneath her lashes. 'You mean you don't feel too good about yourself at the moment?'

'Would you—with an ex-wife and a reluctant fiancée under the same roof, not to mention the rest of them?'

Vivian laughed. 'Heavens, no! That's one reason why I can't believe this is for real. Not me,' she hastened to assure him, 'but the rest of it. I think she still loves you,' she added, suddenly more than sober.

'Is that what she told you on the jetty?'

'Yes—no. I mean only because I asked her.'

'That's my Vivian,' he murmured wickedly, and put his hand over hers on the rock. 'But why would you do that when you're determined there's nothing real between *us*?'

'Heaven alone knows,' she confessed after a moment. 'I guess curiosity got the better of me.'

'You ran away last night.'

She shrugged. 'Better than falling into a river.'

'What exactly do you think you were running away from, Vivian?'

She sighed suddenly. 'You. This whole situation. I think it got too much for me. But surely it would too much for most people to handle?' She raised an eyebrow at him.

'So you decided you'd still go on as a rent-a-girl in spite of all that?' he queried with irony.

'I haven't got Clover Wines under my belt yet, Lleyton,' she reminded him. 'But while I may be a rent-a-girl in certain respects,' she warned, as she literally started to tingle with annoyance, 'I would advise you not to take any liberties.'

'Is that why you're wearing a shirt over your bikini?' he drawled.

'Yes!' she shot at him. 'I've seen what you can do to a Thai silk suit. Who could blame me for guarding *you* against yourself?—i.e. your harem stroke sultan-like tendencies!'

'Not to mention you,' he murmured, then started to laugh.

'What are you laughing about?' she asked frustratedly.

'My dear Vivian,' he said wryly, 'neither that T-shirt nor your bikini, now they're wet, are offering any protection against anything.'

She looked down, following his gaze. Her white T-shirt, which was perfectly opaque when dry, was now about as transparent as a piece of tissue paper and moulded to her figure like a second skin. Nor was her bikini beneath it hiding the curves of her breasts or the outline of her nipples.

She closed her eyes in utter frustration and pulled the cotton away from her skin. 'I had no idea,' she said. 'But I can assure you this shirt will go to the charity shop as soon as I get home!'

This time he really laughed.

'Lleyton,' she warned through her teeth.

'Vivian, I'm sorry. But it wasn't what I was expecting and I believe you,' he said, still smiling. 'Look, take it off. You're quite safe. I'm not in sultan mode,' he added quizzically.

'Thank you, but I'll leave it on all the same. There is the sun to think about.'

'As you please.' He folded his arms. 'It doesn't stop me from telling you that your figure is perfectly in proportion. You have a straight back, delicious hips, long slim legs, a small waist, very fine ankles and wrists, delicate straight shoulders and small but firm and jaunty breasts. Your skin is smooth and lightly tanned pale gold.'

Her lips had parted during this catalogue of her body, and stayed parted for a long moment after he'd finished. Then she said, 'If that's not sultan mode I'm a concubine, which I can assure you I am not!'

'I'm sure you'd be a delightful concubine, Vivian,' he remarked casually. 'But before you're tempted to hit me perhaps we should rejoin the party?'

She groaned expressively. 'Do we have to? Couldn't I fake a migraine? It only took us a few minutes to get here, so—'

'Not if you value the Clover Wines account.'

It was like having icy water poured over her. And the fact that it was supremely irrational to feel that way, that she herself had brought up the subject earlier, didn't help in the slightest.

'Lead on then, Mr Clover Wines,' she said tartly, then decided not to wait for him.

But although she beat him back to the boat, getting aboard was not as easy as it looked.

'Damn!' she spluttered as he swam up beside her. 'This stupid ladder of yours keeps disappearing under the boat!'

'There's an art to it, Vivian. Let me go first, then I can help you.'

She had no choice but to agree. It didn't put her in a better frame of mind to see him haul himself aboard in a way that emphasised the sleek strength of his body, although it did make her catch her breath unwittingly. Then he held a hand down to her, and it was his strength rather than the elusive rope ladder that got her awkwardly, in a tangle of arms and legs, back on board, so that she subsided panting into his arms, feeling a fool when he helped her to her feet.

'That's a whole lot harder than it looks,' she said breathlessly.

'It helps to have strong arms and shoulders,' he agreed, and withstood the wash from another boat as it zoomed past, rocking theirs, with his feet planted firmly apart like a tree, she thought, whereas she would have fallen over.

She sighed quietly. Because she was feeling safe again, resting against him, and not only that, was starting to be stirred by the contact, the sort of pre-sensation that her slim wet body would start to flower against his if she stood there any longer. All the same, she was powerless to move, although she knew she was asking for whatever he chose to make of the situation.

He didn't choose to make anything of it. He simply let her go and reached for his T-shirt. And said casually, 'I'll turn my back if you want to change here, or you could do it ashore at the restaurant.'

A shocking little sense of disappointment kept her silent for a moment. Then she said quietly, 'Thanks, but I might need a mirror, so I'll do it ashore.' She put her cap and sunglasses on and sat down.

He started the outboard with a roar, pressed a button to bring up the anchor and turned the boat. They said nothing other than about the things of interest he pointed out and she commented on for the ten minutes it took to arrive at the restaurant—a rustic, wooden building with a broad second floor verandah right above the river, where the rest of the party were already ensconced.

But she did say to him as they approached the jetty, 'Is any of those children yours?'

He looked down at her and she wondered whether there

was a trace of bleakness in his blue eyes. 'No. Ginny miscarried.'

'You're very quiet, Vivian.'

It was Mag. Lunch was finished. It had been a lively meal with—thanks to Amelia—none of the undercurrents about her son's engagement to a complete stranger being allowed to surface. Which, considering her reaction to the pink diamond ring, had been no mean feat of social dexterity.

It had also been an opportunity for Vivian to watch the Dexter family interacting. Ralph had been on his best behaviour, charming and funny, affectionate towards Mag, and he and Lleyton had seemed to have an easy rapport, although they were so different. It had also been obvious that Amelia was revelling in this closeness her three children were exhibiting, and there had definitely been a wry but very fond way her gaze rested on her younger son.

It was the first overture Lleyton's sister had made by coming to sit next to Vivian now, as the party moved about, some going down to water's edge to fish with the children.

Mag was casually attired, like the rest of them, and she was quite a lot like Lleyton, with the same colouring plus the aura of a person who knew her own mind.

'Too much food, sun and that kind of thing,' Vivian replied ruefully, although she could feel the tension rising within her, because she had a good idea of what was to come. 'The food was sensational.'

'Yes, it's always good here. People even fly in on float planes.'

'Thank heavens I didn't have to do that!'

Mag looked at her wryly. 'Lleyton told me how you hate flying.'

Vivian's eyebrows shot up.

'Don't look so surprised,' Mag murmured. 'He is my brother. Why shouldn't he tell me about you?'

'No…reason. Uh—I just feel a bit embarrassed about it—flying, I mean,' Vivian said disjointedly.

And, right on cue, the question Vivian was dreading came. 'How long have you known him?' Mag asked with a frown in her eyes.

'Not very long. It—happened rather suddenly,' she said lamely to Lleyton's sister, then couldn't help herself from adding, 'Look, I'm sorry if it's…been a…disruptive element for you, at this special time. I didn't realise—I mean to say—I had no idea I was about to cause so much trouble,' she finished bleakly.

Mag remained quite still for a long moment, studying Vivian's glum expression minutely. Then she said, 'Eddie likes you and thinks you're good for Lleyton. In fact Eddie was rather annoyed with me for conniving to spring Ginny on him, and although I have a lot of faith in his judgement—' her lips twisted humorously, '—I guess I wouldn't be marrying him otherwise—but he doesn't know how much Ginny loves Lleyton, or… Well, I hadn't met Eddie when Lleyton and Ginny were together, so he doesn't know…how they were.'

Vivian swallowed and couldn't think of a single thing to say.

'I know something catastrophic happened between them,' Mag went on. 'Lleyton can be as hard as nails sometimes. I think from inheriting Clover so young and having to sort the wheat from the chaff, the hangers-on, I mean, and keep it going and so on. But, well, I just thought…' She stopped and shrugged frustratedly. 'I thought it also might help you to know…' She trailed off.

Vivian sat up and unconsciously fiddled with the ring

on her left hand. 'Look,' she said, then paused and prayed for some guidance from *somewhere*. 'Your brother is quite safe with me, Mag. I...won't let him marry me on the rebound from his first wife. Promise.'

Marguerite Dexter blinked. 'How...how can you say that?'

Vivian grimaced. 'I didn't know about Ginny until I got here, so...I guess things will need a bit of a reappraisal. By the way, I'm not a fortune-huntress either.'

'I see,' Mag said slowly, then added unwittingly, 'In other circumstances I'd have liked you, Vivian.'

'That's what your mother said to me. If there's one thing that I earnestly wish for you, Mag, it's that you'll believe me and not let this cloud the run-up to your wedding.' She hesitated. 'I certainly have no intention of engaging in any kind of duel for Lleyton with Ginny or creating any more drama.' She got up. 'I don't know about you, but I need to do something to work off that lunch otherwise I'll be putting on weight!'

Mag rose too, and to Vivian's immense surprise, linked her arm through hers. 'You and me too,' she said wryly. 'I swore I would lose a kilo before the big day. At this rate it will be the other way around! What say I talk Mum out of croquet and we have a tennis comp when we get home? Do you play?'

'I do—sounds like a very good idea.'

'You seem to have won my sister round,' Lleyton remarked as they set off behind the bigger boat. 'How did you do it?'

'I told her you were quite safe with me, Lleyton, and I wouldn't let you marry me on the rebound from your first wife—if that was how things stood.'

His hands stilled on the steering wheel. He looked at her incredulously, then started to laugh.

'Lleyton, you're about to run into another boat,' she warned.

'Sorry.' He corrected his course. 'I might have known it would be something original and ingenious, if not to say essentially Vivian Florey!'

'Thank you.'

'But who suggested I was on the rebound?'

Vivian shrugged. 'She did. But I think she's a whole lot happier about this special week of her life now. And no thanks to you, Lleyton,' she added pointedly.

'If they hadn't taken it upon themselves to meddle in my life, this wouldn't have happened,' he said evenly.

Vivian shrugged again, as if it was nothing to do with her.

'And she believed you?' He looked down at her again, this time sceptically.

Vivian gritted her teeth. 'She believed me—if she did,' she conceded, 'because....' And she recounted her whole conversation with his sister.

'A reappraisal?' He grinned. 'Another cat amongst the pigeons.'

'You didn't expect me to stay on and be the complete villain of the piece?'

'I don't know what I expected,' he said, more to himself than her. 'You were very quiet at lunch.'

'A good way to stay out of trouble, I thought.'

'And nothing to do with our earlier encounter?' he queried.

Vivian licked her lips and lied blatantly. 'No.'

'I was only wondering whether my—lack of being in sultan mode had offended you.'

She glanced at him briefly. 'No. Could I even hope you're cured of me?'

'Not at all,' he murmured. 'It's only that I draw the line at being too obvious.'

They'd been cruising along sedately, but, having delivered this line, Lleyton Dexter eased the throttle forward so the outboard roared and the boat started to plane. Without raising one's voice, it would be difficult to communicate, so Vivian didn't respond.

Instead, she contented herself with wondering sadly whether his words made her feel better or worse. Because she had lied; it had been the difficulty of dragging her thoughts away from their last encounter that had kept her unusually quiet at lunch. Her thoughts along the lines of how he could have affected her the way he had, yet be apparently completely proof against her himself…

The tennis was fast and furious, but not serious, and everyone cooled off in the pool afterwards. Then Amelia announced a barbecue for dinner and gave them a couple of hours' respite.

Vivian lay down on her bed, but her mind was ticking over because of a new development. Was she imagining it, she wondered, or had Ralph and Ginny subtly become a pair? They'd partnered each other in the tennis and won the competition, causing Ralph to catch Ginny up in his arms in a perhaps slightly longer than necessary embrace. And after their swim Ralph had got a pair of bongo drums out, and his rhythm and mastery of them had held all of them spellbound, Vivian included. But the most enthusiastic of them all had been Ginny…

So what did it all mean? she wondered. Would Ginny use Lleyton's own brother to get back at him?

She must have fallen asleep without realising it, because two and a half hours later Lleyton came to find her.

She didn't wake when he knocked, but sat up groggily when he put his head around the door and asked if she was decent. It was quite dark and she was dishevelled and disorientated as he came in and switched on a bedside lamp.

Her hand flew to her mouth as she saw the time on the bedside clock. 'Oh, no! I—'

'It doesn't matter, Vivian,' he said quietly, and pulled up one of the wicker chairs beside the bed.

'Doesn't it?' she asked uncertainly, running her hands through her hair. She'd stripped her bikini off and pulled on her black satin 'happy shirt', as she thought of it, before she'd crawled under the sheet. With no opening down the front, it was quite respectable, and gorgeously embroidered with hibiscus flowers in all shades of pink, but she had nothing on under it and she twitched the sheet up a bit.

'No.' He sat down. 'It's only a barbecue, and you must have been tired to sleep like that.'

'I must have been,' she repeated, still a little dazedly. 'I just didn't realise it. I promised myself half an hour.' She looked down at herself. 'Sorry to receive you like this. I guess everyone is down there somewhere, enjoying themselves?'

He nodded.

She sat back against the pillows. 'Have I done something wrong?'

'What makes you think that?'

She looked at him with a frown. He had blue jeans on and a white T-shirt with a navy collar. 'I just feel…something.'

'I may be slightly jaundiced again, that's all,' he said after a pause. 'Look, is there anything you'd like?'

She blinked.

'To eat or drink, I mean.'

Vivian sat up and stretched. 'I would like nothing so much as a cup of tea and a sandwich then to be able to curl up with my book—but I guess that won't get me Clover Wines, so—'

He reached for the phone on the bedside table, punched one number to get the kitchen and ordered just that—tea and sandwiches.

'So…I don't have to come down?' she asked uncertainly.

He smiled faintly. 'No. You've had a reprieve. And I was going to suggest a reprieve for both of us tomorrow. How long do you need to get ready for a ball?'

Vivian considered. She'd brought a ballgown and it was hanging up all set and ready to go, in a manner of speaking. She looked at her nails, ran her hands through her hair again, but when all else failed her hair-wise, she could put it up. She looked at Lleyton with a spark of mischief. 'Half an hour. Why?'

He returned her look with one of admiration tinged with wicked amusement. 'Vivian, most men would adore you for that alone. Why? Well, there is to be a ball here tomorrow night, and in deference to the preparations for it an easy day has been ordered. I thought we might play hooky.'

'Where?' she said slowly.

'Palm Beach. It's lovely. We could swim in the surf, have lunch, et cetera, and you wouldn't have to field the family until tomorrow night,' he said gravely.

'That is a huge inducement, Lleyton, but—I don't have to fly to get there, do I?'

His blue eyes rested on her, and softened. 'No. We'll go by boat. But don't forget how brave you've become about flying with me.'

Her hands were clasped on the coverlet and she dropped her gaze to them as they involuntarily tightened. Because a day away from the family and the charade of being his fiancée would be sheer heaven. But a day alone with Lleyton Dexter could be another kind of strain and those simple words—*how brave you've become about flying with me*—seemed to encapsulate her dilemma. How to resist him, in other words.

She swallowed. 'I—'

'I promise not to do anything you don't want me to do, Vivian.'

She sighed and looked up at him at last, then couldn't seem to tear her eyes away, and everything that was between them, that magnetic field of attraction she could no longer deny, was out in the open, as her body started to tingle. Not with annoyance, but desire.

And it came to her that to slide down in the bed and welcome Lleyton Dexter beside her, to laugh with this tall, sometimes infuriating, often enigmatic man, to love him, even just to ease whatever it was that was bothering him at the moment—and she was sure there was something—to let him love her would be dangerous, perhaps foolish, asking to get her heart broken. But also heaven.

Then she remembered Ginny and Ralph, and it all seemed to fall into place.

She lowered her lashes abruptly. 'A straight, honourable deal?'

'It would be entirely up to you.'

She shivered.

He moved. 'I'm not Casanova, Vivian.'

'No,' she agreed but a little bleakly. 'OK.'

'Good girl. Ah,' he stood up at a knock on the door. 'Here comes your supper. Sleep well.'

CHAPTER FIVE

'THAT'S the Barranjoey lighthouse,' Lleyton said.

They'd made an early departure from Harvest Moon and it had taken them an hour by boat to reach Pitt Water, where they'd tied up at a marina then transferred to a Range Rover in the car park. It appeared it was a regular arrangement of his to keep a car handy. The Hawkesbury opened into a wide body of water at its mouth, with many inlets and creeks running off it. Palm Beach was on the ocean side of a narrow arm that protected Pitt Water, with Barranjoey Head and its lighthouse standing sentinel.

Vivian had been fascinated by the lovely waters they'd travelled through, the towering cliffs of Ku-ring-gai Chase National Park, Cowan Creek and this second fascinating aquatic playground that was virtually on the city's doorstep, as well as Sydney Harbour; fascinated by all the boats, the lovely little beaches, islands and inlets and residential areas you could only reach by boat. It was also a heavenly day, clear, sparkling and hot.

They'd had a swim in the surf at Palm Beach, with its lively pavement cafés and boutiques, and were now doing a tour of the headland. Throughout the morning Lleyton had been the perfect companion, fun to be with and relaxed, so that she'd unwittingly overcome her reservations about the kind of stress this day would bring.

'Hungry?' he asked as they watched a team of windsurfers launch their colourful sails from a grassy park.

She smiled. 'It is around lunchtime.'

'Then let's eat.'

But it wasn't to a restaurant that he took her. He drove back along the road to Sydney for a few kilometres, then turned into an almost hidden driveway on the ocean side that ran down steeply between a tangle of trees and shrubs, and all that could be seen as they stopped was a wooden garage door that slid soundlessly open at the touch of a remote control device.

'What is this?' she asked.

'It's my retreat. It's probably the one place I call home. Don't,' he said as she tensed visibly, and put a hand over hers. 'I didn't bring you here to seduce you. I wanted you to see it, that's all.'

She looked into his eyes, and they were sober and very blue.

All the same, it was with a slight feeling of wariness that she walked through from the garage into the house, only to be stunned by what she saw. The house was built on the side of a steep cliff down to the ocean and the views were sensational; so was the large room that opened out onto a timber deck.

There were comfortable couches covered in a pale sea-green linen, lovely rugs on the terracotta tiles, trees in earthenware pots scattered around, low brass and mother-of-pearl inlaid chests, statues and carvings and lovely wall hangings. And it flowed out onto a terrace, through a whole wall of glass sliding doors with timber louvers, where there were more potted shrubs and trees, statues and a jarrah setting of table and benches.

But the other thing that struck her about Lleyton Dexter's retreat was the privacy. It was like being in a light, airy cave on the cliffside, remote from all the bustle of Palm Beach and Pitt Water, from the world.

'Well?'

She turned to find him standing behind her, looking down at her quizzically in his stone cargo shorts and maroon shirt. She wore a brief sundress over her bikini and they were both tousled, salty and aglow from the sun.

She shook her head. 'I don't think words can do it justice. It's…lovely.'

'Thanks. Now, if everything went according to plan, my genie should have provided lunch. Let's have a look.'

The kitchen he led her into had the same view and was designed like a ship's galley, with lots of wood and stainless steel appliances. He opened the fridge. 'Yep! She has.' He stood aside for Vivian to look into it.

There was not a lot in it apart from a couple of basics, like butter and milk. But there was a big bowl of cooked but unpeeled prawns, a platter of oysters, two lemons, a smaller bowl of mayonnaise, a salad, a magnificent chocolate cake decorated with nuts and cherries as well as a cheeseboard covered with clingfilm.

Vivian sighed with pleasure.

'You approve?' he queried.

'Who wouldn't? Oysters, then cold prawns to eat with your fingers on a hot day. She's a genius, your genie. How did she know I adore chocolate cake, I wonder?'

'I took a punt there. Just told her to make something for afters,' he said wryly. 'Shall we eat outside? There should be fresh bread too.'

There was. A round brown cob loaf. And between them they assembled a couple of trays and took the meal out to the deck.

'Oh,' Vivian said, and stopped beside the table. 'I don't think I'll come any further.'

Lleyton grimaced and tapped his forehead. 'Forgot about heights. But you know, Vivian, this wouldn't be a lot higher than your third floor apartment. For the meantime, though, we'll stay here.'

'Thanks.' She sat down at the table. 'I'm fine here.'

They started with the oysters, little Sydney rock oysters that were superb with a dash of lemon juice, and he had a beer and made a shandy for her. Then they went on to the prawns; Lleyton peeling and eating his one at a time, Vivian peeling all of hers first before starting to eat them—and laughingly trying to work out what sort of characters this made them.

The sun poured down, so he got them two straw hats, and the sea was blue as far as she could see. There were gulls wheeling, also birds calling in the grevilleas and melaleucas and native bush that grew beneath the deck. There were a couple of white sails on the wrinkled blue of the ocean. The outside of the house was lined with silvery grey weathered western cedar and the roof was shingled so it blended in perfectly with the hillside.

'This is just wonderful,' she said, rinsing her fingers in the finger bowl then drying them on a linen napkin. 'A celebration of the sea, and its food, eating with your fingers, the sun and this part of the world.'

He raised an eyebrow. 'Perhaps we should be drinking wine.'

'No.' She raised her shandy. 'But perhaps I should start designing beer labels. There's nothing like it on a hot day?' She paused and frowned. 'Do you not consider Harvest Moon home?'

'Not really. It was my parents' creation, then my mother's domain after my father died. I think she really made it what it is today as some sort of compensation for losing him.' He shrugged. 'It's fine for family times but otherwise not for me. Mag and Eddie are welcome to live there when the time comes if they want to.'

'What about Ralph?'

'He too, if that's what he wants.' He tossed a prawn head and shell into a bowl and regarded the peeled object in his fingers thoughtfully, then raised his gaze to Vivian. 'But Ralph never spends long there.'

'You and Mag are quite a bit alike, but Ralph is so different. I've got the feeling your mother dotes on him although she feels she shouldn't,' Vivian observed.

Lleyton looked amused. 'Mag and I were born quite close together. I don't think she intended to have any more children until—well, he came along a bit later. And I guess, because he was different, she felt protective towards him.'

'Would…Ginny have liked to live at Harvest Moon?' Vivian asked after a bit of a silence.

'Possibly. Yes, I think she would have.' He shrugged.

'Why did you break her heart, Lleyton? Unless it was the other way around.'

A glint of something she couldn't decipher lit his eyes, then he ate his prawn and reached for another. 'Do I detect Mag or Ginny herself giving you that impression?' he mused.

Vivian refused to be drawn. She said instead, 'I can be a good listener, but only if you'd like to tell me. I'm also not without intuition. For example, last night you were…you were different, and I got the feeling you may have needed to get away today as much as I did.'

Their gazes caught and held, but his was still unreadable. 'Two nights ago you didn't want to know anything about it, Vivian.'

She moved her shoulders restlessly. 'I guess I've thought since then that we could be friends,' she said quietly, staring out to sea. 'But if you don't—'

'Only friends?' he broke in.

'It…' She bit her lip. 'It's a start. It's better than all manner of things being done in the name of Clover Wines, for example,' she added dryly.

His lips twisted. 'Does that mean when you've got the wine account you'll consider a relationship, Vivian?'

Her gaze came back to rest on him and she swallowed. 'I'm…I don't know. I got walked out on once, so, yes, I guess I am a bit bruised.' She stopped and looked at him ruefully. 'I know this sounds crazy, but it would help if you were just the tiniest bit vulnerable in some way yourself. I might not feel as if I were walking into a lion's den, not knowing what to expect.'

Several expressions chased through his eyes. Then he said with a grin, 'There's not the slightest likelihood of getting eaten.'

'I was talking metaphorically!'

'I know.' He was still grinning and pushed his plate away. 'Well—'

But Vivian interrupted as some things suddenly crystallised for her. 'What I meant was you got walked out on too, by the sound of it, even although she does want you back now. So I just wondered if, because you know what it's like, you might know how I feel. Scared stiff of ever letting it happen to me again,' she said with clear, painful honesty. 'And, well, feeling much better off if you don't let yourself rely on other people for your happiness, if you know what I mean.'

Every trace of amusement drained slowly from his expression as he studied her, the way her throat worked, the way her hands clenched, the shadows of torment in her hazel eyes, the taut lines of her figure beneath the short white pique sundress she wore over her bikini.

'How did it happen?' he asked quietly.

'He was someone I worked with at Goodman's. He was the first—' She stopped and bit her lip. 'The first man I'd got really close to. Because I lost my mother so young, and because my father never got over it, and because I lived a very unsettled life as a child,' she explained, 'I became something of a loner and afraid to...' She shrugged. 'Isn't that what Stan told you? He—I sometimes think he knows me better than I know myself.'

'Not exactly,' Lleyton said slowly. 'He told me you were an orphan and that he looked upon you almost as a proxy daughter. He also told me that you could be, well, headstrong in that your enthusiasm for your work sometimes ran away with you. So this man,' he continued, before she had a chance to comment either way, 'let you believe your relationship was heading somewhere then—decamped?'

'Yes. No,' Vivian said with some perplexity. 'I may have read more into it once we started sleeping together. Which is something I wouldn't have done if I hadn't thought—Look...' She paused. 'I obviously did read more into it than he ever intended.'

'Do you still love him?'

'No. If you mean am I miserable, bereft and all the rest, no. Not any more. But at the time I was...pretty unhappy. I guess you always are when it happens that way around.'

Lleyton stared at her for a long moment, then he looked away briefly. 'It was the other way around for me. I gave *her* her marching orders, but in a moment of black humour I told her to let everyone think the opposite.'

Vivian's lips parted, then she took the straw hat off and fanned herself. 'Why?'

'Shall we get rid of this mess and make some coffee to have with our cake first?' he suggested.

'If you like.'

So that's what they did—made a pot of plunger coffee and, because it was really hot on the deck now—hot enough to melt the chocolate cake, he said with a lurking smile—they stayed indoors.

It was Vivian who poured the coffee and cut the cake, and they sat on two settees, drawn up at right angles to each other with a low table between them.

And it was Vivian who said abruptly, 'If you've changed your mind about telling me it's OK.'

He looked at her meditatively, then leant forward to put sugar in his coffee. 'No, I haven't changed my mind. In fact…' He paused. 'Well, it's something I need to do now. I met Ginny through Mag. It was about six years after my father died and I was…' he paused again and stared out over the terrace '…somewhat disillusioned with life.'

'Why?' Vivian watched him over the rim of her coffee cup.

'I guess I hadn't expected or wanted the responsibility of Clover so soon. Not that I'd ever intended to make the airforce a career, but before he died, my father and I had had plans to start an aircraft manufacturing company. That's what I'd really wanted to concentrate on. Not shampoo, wine and the whole shooting match. But it was impossible.'

Vivian waited silently but not impatiently, because she was drinking in new impressions of Lleyton Dexter. Thinking of him coming out of the airforce with a dream in his heart but being presented with an empire to run. Thinking of him as young and carefree then being hardened and shaped by enormous responsibility. *Did* it, she wondered, account for the implacable side of him and the cynicism that even extended to women now?

Yet in his shorts and shirt, with his hair ruffled and awry and his long bare legs, it wasn't so hard to imagine him being a devastating but laughing lover who could have anyone he chose…

'Impossible,' he went on finally, 'because Clover was in a bit of a downspin—because of my father's sudden death and the economic climate of the day more than anything else. It took a lot of work and nerve to stop it from crash landing, talking aeronautically,' he said wryly.

'Are you saying Ginny walked into your life when you were a bit vulnerable?' she asked seriously.

He laid his head back thoughtfully. 'Perhaps. I certainly didn't see I was being targeted as a husband. I was certainly very attracted to her—'

'That wouldn't be hard. She's very…she's unusually beautiful.'

Lleyton raised his head and eyed Vivian quizzically. 'Thank you. Is that supposed to make me feel better? Any man would have had the same problem, kind of thing?'

She grimaced. 'Sorry. Didn't mean to sound patronising.'

He laughed quietly. 'You might not be so far off course, Miss Florey. Anyway, before things…may have got to that stage by a natural progression, we got married, when she discovered she was pregnant. Although technically, it shouldn't have happened.'

Vivian's eyebrows shot up.

'She had told me she was on the Pill. But even the Pill can fail you, or so I believed. What I hadn't been aware of, though, were the dire straits her family was in. They were—are—graziers—'

'So you didn't really know her background?' Vivian broke in incredulously.

'Yes, I did,' he contradicted. 'It's an old family from western New South Wales, and although they weren't personally known to us the name was. And I met them, of course. My mother,' he said a shade grimly, 'was suitably impressed—the Deacon name is enshrined in the First Fleet. I also realised they'd seen better days, but the prospect they were facing of having to walk away from their station empty-handed was a closely guarded secret, and Ginny's mother put up an amazing show right to the bitter end.'

'How did the bitter end come about?' she asked sadly.

'A series of events. Ginny miscarried after we'd been married for a few weeks. She was three months pregnant and according to the doctors it was simply a pregnancy destined to go that way. I wasn't so sure. She'd been…strange as soon as we got home from our honeymoon. Tense and nervous. Then she came to me in tears one day and told me that her father was threatening to commit suicide because of his financial burdens, and begged me to help. I…that's when I started to wonder,' he said flatly.

'What made you do more than wonder?' Vivian asked, sadly again.

'I found her mother's letter. It was unequivocal. Things were desperate, she said, but since Ginny had got me to marry her, and even although she'd lost the baby, surely she was sure enough of me by now to ask me to bail them out?'

'Oh.' Vivian closed her eyes.

'As you say. But to give her her due,' Lleyton said dryly, 'her family, especially her mother, put enormous pressure on her. It is a proud old name, there were three younger brothers all still at school or university, and I guess Ginny herself was staring the loss of prestige, et cetera, in the face.'

'But I don't understand—why are your family on her side?' Vivian asked curiously.

'They don't know what happened,' he said.

'*Did* you bail her family out?'

'Oh, yes. But part of the deal—which they were all only too happy to go along with—was that it should never be made public. Not even to Mag or my family.'

'I see. That's when you told her to tell everyone she had given you your marching orders?'

'As you say,' he drawled again. 'The other part of the deal was that bailing the family out would be the divorce settlement.'

Vivian looked shocked.

'It could have been much worse,' he said with a ghost of a smile. 'But it still doesn't come cheap, discovering you've been duped.'

Vivian looked even more shocked. 'You don't mean to say she would have tried to get more from you!'

'No.' He shrugged. 'But by then I was wary enough to make sure she didn't. You see, by then I'd also found out that the Pill hadn't failed her because she'd never been taking it. That kind of deception, that sort of wilful using of another life to attain one's ends, really got to me. If there was one thing I couldn't forgive, that was it.'

Vivian breathed deeply. 'Just tell me something, though, Lleyton, how did she fool you? Not about the Pill but…about loving you?'

There was silence for a long, long moment, apart from the birds outside and the sea crashing at the foot of the cliff.

'Did she fall in love with you along the way?' Vivian suggested barely audibly.

'So she said.' His words were clipped and curt.

'And have you considered that you two could go to your graves loving each other in spite of what she did?'

'Yes,' he said, and put his empty cup on the chest. 'And

I'm sorry if it's happened for her. But I doubt it, and I know it's not the case for me. Vivian,' he warned as she opened her mouth, 'don't start to lecture me about pride.'

She subsided, but after a moment she did say, 'As your rent-a-girl, I'm entitled to have my doubts, Lleyton. But...' She hesitated as he shot her a sardonic look. 'I...thanks for telling me.'

He eyed her suspiciously.

'Well, you must see that it makes things look a bit suspect,' she said reasonably.

He turned his dark blue gaze away, then back to her, and said with soft satire, 'One of the reasons I'm *renting* you, Vivian, is because I didn't think I'd get you otherwise. Look—' he spread his hands '—it was a spur-of-the-moment thing. For which you have to take some of the responsibility, I'm afraid. From the moment you walked into my office without your shoes I was intrigued.'

'Those shoes—which cost a fortune, incidentally—were never worth a cent and have caused me a whole lot of trouble,' she said with a tinge of bitterness.

'That rather depends on the outcome of it all.'

She shrugged and frowned at him. Because she'd suddenly got the impression that a change had taken place, that he'd slipped into another gear somehow, only she couldn't put her finger on what had caused it. Then it came to her that they'd exchanged confidences of the most personal nature but, instead of putting them on a closer footing, there seemed to be a greater chasm between them that had opened up with his last words.

Words that to her even wiped out the undemanding kind of friendship they'd shared over the morning and lunch. Words that, curiously, seemed to be contrary in spirit to his wanting to show her his ''retreat''. Words, and a mental withdrawal she seemed to sense in him that caused her to shiver inwardly.

Was he regretting being so frank about his disastrous marriage? she wondered. But she'd offered him an out that he'd chosen not to take…

'Vivian?'

She came out of her reverie with a start. 'Sorry—yes?'

'Would you like to have a shower and change before we head back?'

'Uh—yes, thanks.' But again it was like having iced water poured over her, and perhaps it showed, because his eyes softened as they rested on her face, although he looked away almost immediately and stood up.

'I'll show you the guest bedroom,' he said.

She took a long shower in a bid to wash away not only the salt and sand but her strange feeling of being like a grain of sand on the shore, insignificant and alone. Then she pulled on the change of clothes she'd brought—navy shorts and short-sleeved denim shirt. But she'd forgotten a bra, so she had to put her bikini top on again.

She went to sit at the dressing table with her brush in her hand. It was a no frills bedroom, but not in the sense of being cheap or Spartan. There was a sapphire-blue velvety wall-to-wall carpet, and a double bed covered in a severely tailored oyster damask spread with pillows of the same material piped with sapphire. The wooden louvers at the windows, which looked seawards, were enamelled in the same blue, and the built-in dressing table and other furniture were limned wood to match the oyster of the bedspread.

Vivian looked at the reflection of the room in the mirror, and thought that it needed something—something to give it a lift, some life and colour. But then her gaze narrowed on her face and she found herself thinking tormentedly that *she* needed something, a map or a chart to lead her through the waters she was sailing in. A key of some kind to decipher Lleyton Dexter.

He tapped on the door just as she was thinking this, and came in.

And, because it was right on top of her strange thoughts, she couldn't think of a thing to say. She could only look at him now, in the mirror, obviously showered himself, with his hair dark, damp and brushed, wearing clean chinos and a blue and navy checked shirt.

She saw the frown come to his eyes and willed herself to say something light and frothy, but still nothing came. In fact something worse happened. Tears came to her eyes and she had to look down hastily, blinking vigorously, then attack her hair with the brush.

'Vivian?'

'Won't be a minute—my hair!' she said expressively, but sniffed.

He put his hand over hers and took the brush from her fingers then, with his hands on her shoulders, turned her round on the stool. 'What's wrong?'

She opened her mouth to deny that anything was wrong—and started to hiccup. But at least that released her from speechlessness. 'Oh, no! Maybe oysters, prawns and chocolate cake don't—hic!—go so well together.' She closed her mouth and took a very deep breath, but when she released it she hiccuped again, causing her to drop her head into her hands in embarrassment and despair.

'Vivian.' He pulled her to her feet and folded her into his arms, resisting all her suddenly panicky attempts to get away—and the hiccups got worse. 'Be still,' he ordered, and simply held her against him and stroked her hair.

Five minutes later the hiccups had petered out and she took a long, shuddering breath of relief. 'I don't know how you do it, Lleyton, but thanks,' she whispered. 'And I won't worry about my hair. I'll just stick it under my cap—'

He held her away and looked down into her eyes. 'What made you sad?'

'I…' She cleared her throat.

'You were crying—why?'

She closed her eyes and made a faint, husky little sound in her throat as he slipped both hands up to cup her face, a little sound of despair. 'I don't know. It was nothing, really.'

'Tell me,' he said gently. 'Vivian, look at me.'

Her lashes fluttered up and they were wet again. 'I can't,' she breathed. 'I don't really know myself, so…'

'You must have some idea.'

She swallowed. 'I…well, I was feeling like a grain of sand on the shore, you see. Um…sometimes I feel lonely; that's all. It always passes though, so… I was also thinking this room needs brightening up.' She shrugged. 'Just one of those crazy times when I'm the dizzy blonde you first thought I was, I guess.' She tried to smile but it didn't come off, and he said something beneath his breath and started to kiss her.

'Oh, no, please don't,' she murmured as his lips wandered down the side of her face.

'For some reason I can't bear to see you sad,' he responded barely audibly.

'It'll only make it worse,' she answered helplessly, then tensed.

But he took no notice. And he kissed her eyelids and ran his hands down her body and gathered her close. And from then on things ran away with them like an incoming tide on the shore. Sensations she'd only known as a shadowy, faint presentiment of the real thing overcame her with delight so that she could only gasp in wonder. She had no defences to resist them.

The thrill of a big man making her feel so delicate and petite in his arms, the sheer, masculine essence of him to breathe in had the same effect as some heady kind of wine. So it was only natural, after they'd kissed deeply, to stand quite still and unresisting as his long fingers released the buttons of her blouse. They stared into each other's eyes and Vivian felt as if she was drowning in those blue depths, because there was utter absorption with her in them, as if Lleyton Dexter had only one thing on his mind—Vivian Florey.

And it was also powerfully moving for her to feel as if she was the only person existing in the world for him.

He slid the blouse off her shoulders and untied her bikini from behind her neck. And he looked down at last, for a long moment, then up into her eyes again and rested his lips lightly on the corner of her mouth. 'I was right,' he murmured.

She trembled, and his hands moved to cover each breast gently with his palms. 'Actually, I was wrong,' he said against her mouth. 'They're more than I thought they would be, they're exquisite. You are exquisite—so smooth and slender, so delicately curved, yet…' he paused and his fingers moved on her nipples '…so warm and alive.'

She tilted her head back and was swept by the most intense sensations as her nipples flowered beneath his fingers and she slid her arms around his neck. 'I need something to hold on to,' she said huskily. 'That's so nice…'

She closed her eyes as his mouth slid down her neck

and his hands moved down to her hips, setting her on fire with desire. 'Hold on all you like,' he said softly.

'You're like a tree sometimes, you're so strong,' she whispered.

'And you're like a siren, singing me a song I can't resist,' he responded.

Vivian stilled and moved her hands down from his neck to lay them against his chest as she stared into his eyes. Then her gaze faltered and some sanity prevailed, brought back to her by those words. He'd said something similar to her once before. She remembered all too well. About being a temptation towards earthly delights he should be strong enough to resist. And had said it contemptuously, what was more.

Then there was the conviction she'd always held in the dim recesses of her mind that this would be a test. A test to prove her integrity. A test of whether she would be strong enough to resist him even while she needed something from him. But she knew so much more now. The true story of his marriage to Ginny Deacon. And there was, anyway, the bottom line in it all. She'd come close to breaking her heart once—she had even less assurance this wouldn't be another experience of it, only worse…

She flinched inwardly and fumbled for her bikini top and tied it up behind her neck.

'Why?' he murmured, his blue gaze suddenly narrow and probing.

'I…' She cleared her throat. 'I'm definitely not on the Pill, for one thing.'

'There are other ways.'

She swallowed and moved self-consciously in the circle of his arms. 'I know, but I—it was the one thing I swore to myself I wouldn't do to get Clover Wines.'

'Who said anything about wine or Clover?'

'Lleyton,' she sighed, 'I—' But it was impossible to put her tangle of thoughts into words.

He stood looking down at her, still making no attempt to release her, but it was as if another shutter had come down—other than the tinge of mockery in his eyes now. He then chose to explain. 'Who's to say we would have gone much further anyway, Vivian?'

Her face flamed, but indignation started to seethe within her. 'There was not a lot further to go,' she said tautly.

His eyebrow quirked. 'Whoever he was, Vivian, he obviously didn't have much imagination if that's all he taught you and that's what you truly believe. Believe *me*.'

She tried to raise a hand to slap his face but he caught it, folded it into his, shaking his head wryly at the same time. 'Have you no sense of self-preservation, Vivian Florey?'

'You wouldn't...you wouldn't,' she stammered. 'I mean...'

'Retaliate?' he drawled. 'No. Well, not in kind. It would be much nicer, actually, and something I know you're not at all averse to. For someone who used to hate kissing,' he added idly, 'you seem to have made a remarkable turnabout.'

Vivian clenched her teeth, squeezed her eyes shut, then said intensely, as if the words were wrenched from her heart, 'Stop making fun of me, Lleyton Dexter! You're the one who blows hot and cold. You're the one who brought me here and told me about your marriage then shut me out! You're the one who compared me to a siren, as if I was all set to lead you to the rocks. You're the one who told me you should be strong enough to resist the kind of earthly delights I represented. Not to mention being in sultan mode some days and not on others...'

She stopped, breathing heavily and with tears forcing

themselves into her eyes again, despite her willing herself fiercely not to cry. But they came all the same, and she dashed at them impatiently with her wrist. 'I don't know what got into me, but if that's only way to get Clover Wines, then the deal is off,' she finished proudly, despite her streaming eyes.

'Here,' he said, releasing her at last and pulling a large white handkerchief from his pocket. He put his arms loosely around her again while she dealt with the tears and blew her nose and held her breath in case she started to hiccup again. And when she was all mopped up he took her hand, picked up her shirt for her and led her into the lounge. 'Sit down,' he said unemotionally. 'I'll get you something to drink.'

Vivian sank down onto a couch and pulled her shirt on. She was still feeling shuddery with emotion and took the glass of wine he brought gratefully. He'd poured one for himself and went to stand at the glass doors, staring out to sea.

Then he turned and said, 'The problem is, I thought we were two of a kind.'

She looked at him helplessly, took another sip to steady her voice. But it was still gruff as she spoke. 'In what way?'

His gaze roamed over her. 'Able to handle ourselves,' he said at last, sombrely.

Vivian blinked several times. 'I…I'm not sure what you mean.'

'As in two people who are intrigued and attracted but don't necessarily want a long-term commitment.'

'Is that how I came across, Lleyton?' she asked, huskily and incredulously.

He frowned. 'You certainly gave as good as you got.

And you did agree to this.' His glance homed in on the ring on her finger.

Her lips parted but no sound came, and after a moment he came to sit beside her.

She glanced at him through her lashes. 'I…had no intention of sleeping with you. I've told you that—'

'And now you've shown me.' There was some self-directed irony in his voice, but also a spark of sheer devilment in his eyes.

She trembled inwardly and thought of enlightening him as to how close she'd come to it, how it had only been his choice of words that had pulled her from the brink, then thought better of it. 'Uh—and if I gave as good as I got it was only—well, for two reasons. To show you that you weren't irresistible, and—for Goodman's sake.'

She paused, with the words on her lips once again to tell him how desperately they needed his accounts. But once again she couldn't bring herself to say it. And especially not now, after hearing Ginny's story, she thought with a tremor.

'So,' she went on, 'although you might have…wanted me,' she said with difficulty, 'are you saying you never had any kind of commitment in mind?'

'Yes.'

'And…nothing about me has changed your mind?' she asked, unable to hide the pain in her voice.

'Plenty about you has—endeared you to me,' he replied. 'That's why I'd hate to hurt you.'

Vivian breathed deeply and discovered that she felt as if she'd been turned inside out, exposed in every detail and left shivering and naked. She said with a tremor, 'What made you change your mind?'

'The way you've been. A fighter almost to the end. And what you told me earlier today, which explains why you've fought me even when it's been mutually electrifying between us at times.' He fiddled with the ring on her finger. 'A girl who got her heart broken, Vivian?' He looked into her eyes suddenly.

'Yes,' she whispered, unable to look away, then smiled painfully. 'That's why I was so sure I could handle you, Lleyton. I was wrong, but part of my problem was…I feel amazingly safe with you at times. And not so much of an idiot who's scared of flying, heights and lifts, who gets hiccups, falls into rivers, loses her shoes and all the rest.'

He let her hand go but put his arm around her shoulder and lay back with her. 'It's also why I told *you* the truth about Ginny,' he said. 'I'd decided, at lunch, it was time we called this whole business off—well, after tonight. And I thought the least I owed you was an explanation. My good intentions weren't quite proof against seeing you look so bereft, however.'

She said with a tremor, 'Are you…sworn off commitment now because of Ginny?'

'Yes and no. I suppose, after Ginny, it's natural to be wary, but the real problem is I'm the wrong kind of man for a girl like you, Vivian.'

'As in…how?' she queried.

'I think the last thing you need is a man who's on the move the way I am, especially now my dream is about to come true.'

She looked confused, then suddenly enlightened. 'The aircraft factory?'

'Mmm. It's going to take most of my time for the next few years.'

She stared into his blue eyes and for a terrible moment was assailed by so much about this man: the memory of being in his arms, the way he could ignite her like no other and bring her to a trembling state of desire with so light a touch, the way they could laugh and be easy together… So that now it was as if her world had collapsed around her like a house of cards.

Which forced her to face the fact that Lleyton Dexter had been both so very right for her and so very wrong. Otherwise she wouldn't be feeling like this: sad, with an intimation of a dire loneliness to come—and rejected.

'OK?' he asked quietly.

Damn you, Lleyton Dexter, she thought, with tears in her eyes again. Here she was, sitting with her head on his shoulder yet again and her heart breaking, and he could ask that… Where was her spirit, her pride? How could she retrieve them? How could she end this for once and for all?

'Yes,' she said gruffly. 'Well, I guess one would be foolish to think they could compete. If it was anything else but planes,' she said humorously, and sat up as *something* came to her rescue—pride, possibly, but she was in no position to question it, 'I might have stood a chance. But, well, yes, I do see now!' And she wondered whether he had any idea that she was trying to retrieve her dignity, her whole world, with this kind of bravado.

He looked at her meditatively, but before he could speak she got another idea. 'By the way, I'd rather not come to the ball tonight. I think you're right; we should end this now for once and for all.' And she pulled his ring off and handed it to him decisively.

He rolled it between his fingers, studying it with a faint frown. 'So—no regrets?' he asked, looking up abruptly into her eyes.

She gestured casually. 'A couple. But I'll get over them.' She smiled at him jauntily. 'And to be honest it'll be a relief to—well, get back to sanity, if you don't mind me saying so. From the moment I met you I've felt like

Alice in Wonderland, or as if I'd strayed into a mad-house,' she added ruefully.

Something flickered in his eyes, but all he said was, 'Your things are at Harvest Moon.'

'Oh.' She looked down at herself frustratedly, then brightened. 'Perhaps I could stay here for tonight, or somewhere in Palm Beach, and you could send my things over tomorrow? I could get myself home with no problem, truly.'

'I'd rather you came to the ball.'

She stared at him and was suddenly reminded of how he'd been the night they'd had dinner in Brisbane, reminded of the other, the tough, cool side of Lleyton Dexter. 'But why?'

He shrugged. 'There's still Clover Wines.'

'What?'

'You haven't quite got it yet, Vivian, and I happen to know how desperately Goodman's needs it.'

She could only stare at him, with supreme shock and outrage clearly written in her expression.

'Having lost some of your biggest accounts recently,' he continued expressionlessly.

'You knew! All the time you *knew*,' she accused in a hoarse whisper.

He shrugged. 'Yes. What difference does it make?'

Vivian stood up and stared down at him. 'Do you mean to tell me you've known all along the *real* reason I've participated in this ridiculous charade, Lleyton?' she ground out.

'One of the reasons, yes,' he drawled. 'Another reason was that you couldn't help yourself.'

'Can I tell you something?' she said jerkily. 'It was the *only* reason I didn't walk out of your office when you first mentioned girls and peaches—'

'You had no shoes either,' he reminded her wickedly.

'That was neither here nor there! I'd have walked back to Brisbane in my bare feet if it hadn't been for Goodman's!'

'Well, Vivian,' he murmured, 'here's your chance to really save the agency. I would have thought a ball would be a pleasure compared to walking to Brisbane in your bare feet.'

Vivian swallowed and couldn't recall being more infuriated, deceived or powerfully motivated to retaliate. How could a man make her feel the way he had? How could he sit there, having exposed her innermost self and rejected her, then do this to her…?

She took a deep, trembling breath. 'Don't think I don't know why you're doing this, Lleyton,' she said coolly.

His eyebrow quirked, but other than looking amused he merely waited for her to go on. All the tall, strong length of him—all the things she thought she'd come to love about him, she admitted to herself with stark honesty—those deep blue eyes, that lazy smile, his strength and his gentleness, the feeling of security he gave her, being the only person in the world who could get her to fly with him and stop her nausea and hiccups… But now this.

She closed her eyes briefly. 'I'll tell you. You need a buffer zone tonight, don't you, Lleyton? In case this ball exposes you to Ginny—at her most stunning. But not only that—in case it exposes you to your ex-wife using your *own* brother to make you jealous.'

Their gazes locked together for an age, hers fiery bright, his completely dispassionate. But then, when had she been able to read his eyes when he didn't want her to? she reminded herself.

'Do you think I didn't get those vibes yesterday?' she

went on, 'Do you think I didn't realise it was why you needed to get away today?'

He stood up to tower over her, but Vivian didn't back so much as a step away. 'Could you even be planning to use me to make *her* jealous in a game of tit-for-tat tonight, Lleyton?' she went on. 'Why don't you just come out and say it? Then I'd really know where I stand.'

CHAPTER SIX

'YOU may stand wherever you care to stand, Vivian,' he said softly, but in a way that was lethal enough to send a shiver down her spine. 'If you want Clover Wines, however, you'll come back to Harvest Moon with me tonight.'

'And...and then?'

He smiled at her through his teeth. 'Then I'll consider the deal done.'

'But...' She paused, then was amazed to hear herself say, 'What about the rest of the time leading up to the wedding?'

He looked at her sardonically. 'Are you proposing to aid and abet me in perpetuating the scenario you've just flung at me right up until Mag gets married? That is...more sacrificial than I expected. Unless—' He stopped and watched her narrowly. 'You aren't angling for more of the Clover accounts, by any chance, Vivian?'

She bit her tongue on the flow of colourful language that sprang to mind at the same time as she resisted another urge to slap his face.

But she did say, after lightning thought, 'Never entered my mind. But now you mention it—why not?' She eyed him ingenuously. 'Because, to be honest, what's the point of making her jealous for a night then sending me home with my tail between my legs? I could even do a better job of it now I know what it's all about. Really give her a run for her money if that's what you want. You see—'

'Vivian,' he warned roughly.

'Just let me finish. You see, I'm quite prepared to admit

that I haven't been much good at my prescribed role so far, but then I was casting around in the dark, so to speak.' She smiled, but he was not to know it was an enraged smile. 'Oh, yes, Lleyton, now I know so much more I could even put on another Oscar performance!'

She saw his shoulders move abruptly and tensed in spite of herself, although her hazel gaze never left his. Then she saw him relax visibly, and didn't know that a little pulse at the base of her throat beat a rapid tattoo of relief. But if she was relieved to know he was no longer deeply angry, there was also a kind of crazy elation in knowing she had made him angry. Yet she found herself holding her breath as she wondered what was to come…

'All right,' he said dryly. 'Clover Wines for an Oscar-winning performance tonight. Then we might discuss things further. But, in fact, I had decided to have myself called away on business for the rest of the run-up to the wedding. Mag would never have forgiven me for missing this ball, it's be to the highlight of the week, but she'd understand the next few days.'

'Oh.' For a moment Vivian couldn't help looking crest-fallen, which made her feel ridiculous, and more so when he laughed softly at her expression.

'Are you feeling hoist with your own petard?' he enquired lazily.

'Hoist with something,' she responded tartly. 'But you started this.'

'For my sins, so I did.' But his expression was as coolly amused as it had ever been as that enigmatic blue gaze roamed over her. 'Ready?'

Vivian clenched her fists and opened her mouth. But once again Stan Goodman rose in her mind's eye, and once again it stopped her from flinging Clover Wines in Lleyton Dexter's face. 'Yep!'

'Don't forget your ring,' he murmured, and handed it back to her.

In fact she had two hours to get ready for the ball.

The trip home had been swift—no sightseeing this time—and mostly silent. And there was such a bustle of activity going on at Harvest Moon she was able to escape to her room without encountering anyone who wanted to stop and chat to her, and able to sink onto the bed and thank heavens she had a couple of hours, because she felt, literally, as if she'd been through a wringer.

Not only that, she thought with some despair as she lay back, but she was kicking herself for what she'd done, the things she'd said.

She turned over, slipped her hand under her cheek and stared into space.

She wondered who could blame her, though. Because Ginny Deacon had been right. Falling in love with Lleyton Dexter was asking to get your heart broken. What would have happened, for example, she asked herself, if they had made love today? Would she have got Clover Wines and a pat on the head? Was she ever going to get Clover Wines without sleeping with him?

She moved restlessly and wished devoutly that no such thing as the wine account or Goodman & Associates existed, because they only clouded the issue and only ever could. On the other hand, she'd been so sure that to resist sleeping with Lleyton was the right and ethical thing to do on a business and a personal plane. It must surely have been a deep-seated conviction to have pulled her up in the midst of such physical rapture, half-naked in his arms and loving it, she thought dismally.

But if you did dispense with the wine account, if you

just admitted you'd fallen in love with Lleyton Dexter, she also asked herself, what hope was there for you?

She sat up abruptly, frowning in an effort to clear her mind. And it came to her that while she could separate business from the personal issues, whilst she could admit that she would have fallen in love with him anyway—she paused in her internal monologue and trembled to think of it—could *he* ever separate the two, especially after Ginny Deacon?

Or was he the kind of man who genuinely didn't want to commit to anyone? Or— Of course, she thought with an inward little sigh like autumn leaves falling within her soul, leaving her bare, naked and exposed again, it was all much simpler. He still loved Ginny… Despite everything.

She sniffed and reflected ruefully as she scrubbed at her eyes that she'd shed more tears today than in the last few years. But it was the obvious explanation. It was what she'd thrown at him only an hour or so ago, and it explained why she was still at Harvest Moon.

Which presented her with another awful dilemma, she mused, as she got up wearily and went to run a bath. And as she lay in the bath a little while later, with bubbles up to her neck and her hair tied in a knot, she thought more, and deeply, about Ginny Deacon.

She couldn't admire the woman, she decided. And not only because she'd trapped Lleyton but because she was using Ralph. Who was she, however, to judge another woman who'd fallen in love with Lleyton Dexter? Because she was pretty sure that was what must have happened. Who was she to judge the pressures Lleyton himself had acknowledged could have been brought to bear on Ginny? And if they loved each other despite it—all the more—who was she to act as judge and jury? She couldn't have been more kindly yet firmly rejected today when you came to think of it, if you could bear to think of it… And for an aircraft factory.

So what on earth was she going to do tonight? she wondered a little feverishly, then sat up in the bath abruptly, her eyes widening.

'It would surely lose you Clover Wines,' she said aloud to herself.

'And it's about time you faced the fact that Clover Wines have placed you in an impossible position and time you got really moral and ethical, Vivian Florey,' she answered herself. 'Anyone would think it was the only advertising account in the world! Oh, what a fool I've been,' she marvelled, and lay back.

The dress was pure silk, a pale shell-pink. It was strapless, cut straight across the top of her breasts, and fitted smoothly over her waist and hips, then belled out to be gathered in just above her ankles. The silk was rich and sensuous, the style divine, emphasising the litheness of her figure, and with it she wore the only jewellery she possessed, although rarely wore—the single short strand of chunky pearls that had belonged to her mother and she'd had restrung so they were set apart on the finest silver strand.

Her shoes, plain court shoes with little heels, were covered in the same silk. Her hair was tied back in a knot—which she would have done anyway, she decided, because it made her look different and a little mysterious, and she certainly wanted to be a different person tonight. And when Belinda came on an errand to see if Miss Florey needed any assistance, she borrowed some make-up from the girl.

Belinda was delighted, not only to run away to get her

make-up purse, but to help Vivian apply it. In the end, with a very light touch, Vivian only used some taupe eyeshadow, the merest suspicion of blusher and a pinky bronze lipstick.

'You look so different,' Belinda enthused, then frowned. 'Not better, I mean, but grander.'

'Good. It is a ball, after all. So—what do I do now?' Vivian looked at herself once more in the mirror, then straightened her shoulders and took a deep breath.

'Everyone is assembling in the conservatory—the house party, that is—for cocktails, before the other guests arrive. That's where the buffet supper is laid out, and the dancing will be on the terrace outside the conservatory. Thank heavens it's a fine night; Mrs Dexter seems to be able to organise even the weather.'

Vivian suffered a momentary spasm of nerves. It occurred to her that she liked both Amelia and Marguerite Dexter but they might not like her shortly. Then she shrugged and remembered both their qualified comments on the subject of herself. She also reminded herself that what she might achieve tonight appeared to be their heart's desire, so…

'OK, I'm ready,' she told Belinda. 'Thank you so much for helping me!'

'It's a pleasure, miss—oh, don't forget your ring!' She picked it up from the dressing table and handed it to Vivian, who looked down at it, swallowed, and slid it on to her finger for the last time.

The conservatory was aglow with candlelight and the house party, resembling a flower garden of colours, was all gathered when she arrived.

Amelia was in a slinky, glittery daffodil gown, Mag was looking radiant in apple-green. Cousin Mary wore fuchsia pink, one bridesmaid was in raspberry tulle, the other in lavender blue silk georgette, and Lady Wainright wore magenta and was dripping with diamonds. Only one of the distaff side of the house party was not colourful. Which was not to say she wasn't stunning, perhaps the most stunning of them all.

Ginny Deacon had chosen black. A fitted black gown that showed off a sensational figure, with a low-cut bodice held up by narrow diagonal bands linking to a circlet around her neck of silver sequins so her shoulders were bare. At the back, the dress had a tiny train edged with silver, she wore very high, elegant black sandals, her hair was intricately piled up and she had a close-fitting diamond bracelet on one wrist.

The overall effect—black against her extreme fairness, her height, her carriage, the superb fit and cut of the dress, the lovely lines of her figure—was one of almost regal beauty.

Vivian found herself feeling rather small and insignificant in comparison, which was not a bad thing, as it turned out, because it brought out her fighting spirit. She accepted a champagne cocktail from the waiter, and went forward to join the group with her head held high.

Lleyton was there, as was Eddie, both in conventional black tuxedos and snowy white shirts, but Ralph had chosen a maroon suit and matching shirt with a silver cummerbund. All he lacked, Vivian thought, with his ponytail and earring, was a sombrero hanging down his back.

As they all turned at her approach, she said, 'Hi! You do all look lovely. Especially you, Ralph!' She raised her glass to him.

Out of the corner of her eye she saw Lleyton frown faintly but she went demurely to stand at his side. And 'demure' was the best way to describe her demeanour for the next two hours as the guests started to arrive and the buffet supper got under way.

She sat next to him to eat, but little intimate conversation was exchanged. Ginny and Ralph were at the same table, but there were also four other couples, so it was possible if not exactly to ignore him, then certainly possible not to cross swords with him either. Also possible to observe his brother and his ex-wife, and feel her resolve hardening. For Ginny Deacon was aglow and vibrant and very lovely, as if she had not a care in the world, and Ralph was being unusually attentive.

Then Lleyton said, when the dessert was removed, 'Is this what you call winning an Oscar, Vivian?'

'I haven't started that yet.' She sipped her coffee.

'So you plan to go from not talking to me to—the opposite?' He raised an eyebrow at her, but there was something narrow and probing in his blue eyes as his gaze ran over her bare flesh above the lovely pink silk.

'All in good time,' she murmured. 'I just need to wind up, so—'

'You look different,' he broke in. 'I don't think I've ever seen you wear make-up before.'

'Ah—I don't. But this is a ball. I didn't think you'd notice, anyway.'

'It was one of the first things that struck me about you,' he murmured. 'How natural you were.'

'Oh.' Vivian looked at him wide-eyed in surprise for a moment, then looked away a little awkwardly.

'As a matter of fact, I prefer you natural,' he added thoughtfully.

'You don't own me, Lleyton,' she said, out of a sense of injury and being made to feel as if she'd committed some gross indiscretion such as painting herself like a tart.

'No? I was beginning to think I could, body if not soul.'

There was sheer irony in his eyes. 'But the reason I prefer you natural is because it adds to the curious mystique of one Vivian Florey. Would you care to dance? You may not have noticed it but the band has struck up on the terrace.'

'Certainly.' She pushed her coffee away and stood up.

But outside on the terrace, in his arms and fitting her steps to his in a sedate foxtrot, she said, 'You seem to forget the one thing I won't do to get Clover Wines, Lleyton. Now, if you'd said you were beginning to think you could own me in a commercial sense, I might have agreed, but what you actually said is not true.'

They danced in silence for a minute or more, which was a sore trial to Vivian, but she was very angry and that gave her the courage to ignore what being in his arms did to her. And to be almost able to ignore the way his gaze held hers, then dropped deliberately to her breasts beneath the pink silk so that it might just as well have not been there, and she was right back with him in his house at Palm Beach, clinging to him half-naked...

Then he drawled, 'Forgive me for harbouring certain suspicions, Vivian, but I can't help wondering whether we have a carrot and donkey situation here. Your gorgeous body being the carrot and me being the donkey,' he elucidated.

She stopped dancing, but he propelled her backwards so she had to get into step with him again, and said with plain mockery, 'You disagree?'

'Yes.' It came out clipped and curt, but only caused him to smile satanically down at her.

'Then what is it exactly?'

She swallowed. 'Well, funnily enough, I had the same suspicions. That I was going to have to trade my body for Clover Wines despite your assurance of a fair and honest deal, but perhaps I was wrong.' She shrugged.

This time he stopped dancing. 'Perhaps. One thing I wouldn't advise you to forget, however, is how you do tend to—forget yourself at times.'

'What's that supposed to mean, Lleyton?' she asked in a furious undertone.

'That I wouldn't take the carrot bit too far, if I were you, Vivian. That's all. Because I'm beginning to revise my opinions of a bruised girl who got her heart broken. I'm beginning to think Goodman & Associates is far more important to you than anything else.'

She flinched visibly, causing him to smile and lift her hand with his ring on it to his lips. But she did say, barely audibly, 'If there was ever a case of the pot calling the kettle black, that is it.'

'Possibly,' he agreed, 'But I have nothing to lose. In the meantime, there are a few duty dances I need to get out of the way, and I'm sure you won't lack for partners.' He was still holding her hand, and to anyone looking on it would appear that he was being gallant as he touched his lips to it again. 'Let's say we get together again shortly, and perform whatever you have in mind for next instalment of this thrilling saga.'

Her eyes were brilliant as she pulled her hand, still in his, towards her, and kissed his knuckles. 'Why ever not, Mr Clover Wines? why ever not?'

'Ralph?'

Ralph turned from watching Ginny Deacon dancing with a tall, silvery-headed man. 'Ah. The fiancée,' he said genially. 'How goes it, Vivian? I see you haven't lost the ring yet.'

'No. It's a wonderful evening, isn't it? I'm really

thirsty, though.' Vivian sank down at a small table for two and after a moment Ralph sat down opposite her, and as a white-coated waiter passed clicked his fingers and took two glasses of champagne from the tray proffered.

There were fairy lights strung in the trees and burning braziers around the rim of the dance area. The band was on a dais, and as she watched, Mag danced by with Eddie, obviously having the time of her life. The floor was thronged with dancers now, some wearing balloons tied to their wrists, and above it all what could have been called a harvest moon swam in a midnight-blue sky.

Vivian sipped her champagne and sighed.

Ralph cocked his head. 'Where's Lleyton? Don't tell me he's abandoned you?'

'No. He's doing his duty dances. Well…no…um… Ralph, lovely as this is—' she gestured to the dance floor '—the music could be a bit livelier, don't you think?'

Ralph started to frown, as if his antennae had received a slightly off-key signal, but a sudden glint lit his grey eyes. 'You would like it livelier, Vivian?'

She eyed him over the rim of her glass. 'Ralph, I have music in my feet—especially Latino music. I wanted to be a disco dancer as a kid; my main ambition. I thought you might—I don't know why—but I thought you might be the same,' she added softly.

Ralph went to say something enthusiastic, stopped himself, and the frown came back. 'You and Lleyton wouldn't have had a disagreement by any chance?'

Vivian hesitated, lowered her lashes and recalled every word Lleyton had said to her on the dance floor. 'Not at all,' she denied, looking up suddenly and directly into Ralph's eyes. 'Don't tell me you didn't always know I was a rent-a-girl?'

Ralph could only stare at her speechlessly.

'Well, the deal has ended; it was only ever a business deal,' Vivian went on with a shrug, 'but I don't see why I shouldn't go out with a flourish. And—' she sobered suddenly '—it would give you a chance to disengage yourself from Ginny for the evening, because that, I'm sure, is hitting below the belt. He is your *brother* and she was his *wife*.'

'Let me get this straight,' Ralph said cautiously. 'We—you and I—put on a bit of a show for everyone tonight, Ginny is left without a prop, so is Lleyton, and…is that what you're trying to do?' he asked incredulously. 'Bring them back together?'

'It's what your mother, your sister and Ginny herself would appear to want, although I can't go along with her means,' Vivian said candidly, and Ralph actually blushed.

'I guess it's hard living in the shadow of such a successful older brother,' Vivian said quietly.

'You're not wrong,' Ralph agreed bitterly, then looked at her speculatively. 'Something doesn't quite gel about this, Vivian. Why do I get the feeling I could be falling from the frying pan into the fire?'

'I'm not asking you to take up with me, Ralph. Just dance with me tonight,' she said straightly. 'I'm the essential career girl, so, sorry, but there couldn't be any more to it. What's more,' she went on, 'why don't you put your heart and soul into your music, and even if it isn't successful in the Dexter tradition, tell yourself they're Philistines anyway? Because the way you played those drums yesterday talked to my soul, and one day you'll get it together, you see.'

'Do you really mean that?'

'Yes, I do,' she assured him. 'But, in the meantime, why don't you have a word with the band?'

'All right. But if we both get taken out at dawn and shot, just remember this was your idea,' Ralph Dexter said ruefully.

They started their act discreetly, but as the band got livelier, to the delight of three-quarters of the guests, who were Mag and Eddie's ages, it became obvious for all to see that Vivian and Ralph were the item of the evening.

'Boy, you do have music in your feet,' he said to her once. 'Believe me, you'd have been wasted on Lleyton, Vivian!' He put his hands round her waist and carried her shoulder-high across the floor as other dancers parted and started to clap at their sheer expertise. Then he put her on her feet, turned and stalked away in true Latin style, with his hands on his hips. Whereupon Vivian danced after him and tapped him on the shoulder, then stalked away herself with her skirt held in her hands. Everyone loved it.

Almost everyone. Since opportuning Ralph, Vivian had dodged Lleyton, so that she and his brother had come together for every dance for the last hour. They'd also laughed and talked together animatedly, and, as two excellent dancers, very soon established a rhythmic rapport. Then they'd disappeared for twenty minutes, only to take a breather and a long, soft drink and to chat amiably about music, before Trini Lopez's old favourite 'La Bamba' had drawn them back to the floor. And without laying a finger on each other they'd given an exhibition that once again had had the other guests drawing to the edge of the floor and clapping them on.

At the end, Ralph had picked her up high in his arms and kissed her enthusiastically and told her she was sensational.

And just the sheer pleasure of the music and a good

partner had caused her to glow and laugh, and kiss him back.

It was soft, dreamy music that followed and Vivian and Ralph, still dancing together but quietly, caught their breath. It was also when, like a montage, the Dexter family revealed themselves to Vivian: Amelia looking outraged and shocked while Lady Wainright, sitting beside her friend, cast Vivian a look of chilling scorn as she glided past. Mag and Eddie, dancing, but talking seriously and a little frantically. Ginny Deacon, standing alone beside the floor, still tall and regal and ice-cool, but as their gazes clashed for a moment, Vivian saw sheer naked fury in the other girl's eyes.

Serves you right, Ginny, she thought, but I don't know what you're angry about. I've opened up the floor for you and Lleyton… Unless you just don't like losing the limelight or being upstaged in *any* way.

But it was Lleyton himself, whom she'd ignored and evaded for the past nearly three hours, who made her pause and almost trip in fright as they danced past him. He was leaning against a verandah pillar with his arms folded and his expression wasn't enigmatic at all. Those deep blue eyes were full of the most scorching contempt, directed squarely at her.

'Ralph,' she said, and was horrified to discover her voice was a bit wobbly, 'c-can I rely on you to behave yourself for the rest of the night?'

Ralph looked down at her quizzically. 'What do you mean?'

'Well, I think I've done enough damage…um…or whatever, for one night, so I'm going to bed. But I need you to promise you won't get up to any mischief with Ginny.'

Ralph started to protest, but she overrode all his objections about the night still being young, although it was past midnight, how well they danced together, with one point. She told him it was his sister Mag's night and he was duty-bound to retrieve it for her as best he could.

'Promise me those two things,' she insisted.

In the end he did, and Vivian slipped away from him, although she hovered for a while out of sight of any of the family just to see what happened.

Ralph didn't disappoint her. He went straight up to Mag, took her away from Eddie, made a signal to the band, and very shortly they were doing the Charleston expertly, and Mag was laughing and loving it as everyone joined in.

Vivian sighed with relief and turned away. But as she passed through the conservatory, she heard someone say, 'Who is she? The girl in pink?'

'Thought she was Lleyton's property, but there was a bit of a mystery about it. Guess she must belong to Ralph, though…' came the reply.

Vivian bit her lip and ran through the house and up the stairs.

Her bedroom was in darkness and she didn't switch on the light, although she fumbled for the key and locked the door, then leant back against it with several deep breaths as she fought her instinct not to draw attention to herself even by turning on a light. In fact, her instinct was not to draw attention to herself in any way. In fact her instinct was to pack and slip away from Harvest Moon right away, but how? she wondered. Thumb a lift with one of the guests?

She shook her head and picked her way across the room towards the verandah then stopped as if shot as a lamp sprang on. It was the lamp on the table between the two wicker chairs in one corner and it revealed Lleyton, in one of the chairs, with his tie undone, his jacket off, his legs stretched out and a drink in one hand.

She put her hands to her thudding heart and closed her eyes. 'You gave me such a fright! What are you doing here?' Her lashes flew up. 'How did you know I was coming up?'

'I didn't.'

She swallowed. 'So…how long did you plan to stay here?'

'As long as it took,' he drawled.

'But…but this is my bedroom,' she stammered. 'You have no right to be here!'

'This is my house,' he replied. 'Where's Ralph? I hope you didn't have some devious plan for him to climb up the drainpipe? He could injure himself.'

'Climb…what are you talking about?' She stared at him. 'You don't imagine…you don't for one minute think…'

His blue gaze stripped her naked, then he took a leisurely swallow of his drink and put it down on the table and sat forward. 'You were the one who told me about your Latin lovers, Vivian. And now I quite see what you mean. But he can get here by just coming through one of the other bedrooms and along the verandah. Is that the plan?'

Vivian took a few unsteady steps and sank down onto the end of the bed. 'No. Um…no. There is no plan. Not that kind of a plan anyway.'

Lleyton smiled grimly. 'I felt sure there was some kind of a plan, but I gather this is a Vivian Florey special. Do enlighten me,' he invited.

'Lleyton…' She moistened her lips. 'What may have looked like a rebuff to you tonight was in fact something quite different—I take it that's why you're a little put out?' She glanced at him anxiously and her heart started to beat heavily again at the hard line of his mouth.

'Wouldn't you be?' he murmured. 'You're wearing my ring yet you've given the whole world to understand it's my brother you're interested in—'

'I'm not!' she protested. 'And the only reason I'm wearing your ring is because—well, you know why!'

'Yes,' he agreed. 'It's part of a deal we had. In exchange for posing as my fiancée you were to get Clover Wines. The only thing you posed as tonight, Vivian, was a tramp—'

She flew off the bed and faced him with her hands on her hips, 'Don't you dare—'

But he cut her off. 'And maybe posing is the wrong word. I would say it came from the heart; that's how natural you were at it, Vivian.' He stood up.

'Is that so?' she said through her teeth. 'Well, let me tell you I had a great time tonight! And if you think I'm any worse than your ex-wife, you're mistaken, Lleyton Dexter. If looks could kill, the one she sent me a little while ago should have buried me six feet under. I wonder why? Could it be that Ralph dispenses a much better time than you do?' she flung at him, with the light of battle sparking in her eyes.

'Let's put it to the test, then,' he drawled, and put his hands on her shoulders.

'Lleyton—you wouldn't,' she breathed, her eyes now wide with uncertainty.

'Oh, yes, I would, Vivian. Isn't that why you flung down the gauntlet, anyway?' His fingers moved caressingly on her skin.

'No! Oh, no!' A dim sense of the havoc she might have created tonight began to seep into her consciousness and cause her eyes to be horrified, although she was aware that it just didn't seem to fit together.

But he ignored her words, and the look in her eyes, and kissed her forehead.

She closed her eyes and stood straight and impassive beneath his hands and those wandering lips. Nor did she move as he unpinned her hair and ran his fingers through it.

'That's better,' he said, and took her chin in his hand.

Her lashes fluttered up.

'And I like you better now the make-up has worn off, but I think I mentioned that earlier. The dress, on the other hand, is lovely. All the same—would you like to take it off or shall I?' he queried.

Her lips parted incredulously. 'You're not serious?' she whispered.

His eyebrow quirked. 'Oh, yes, Vivian.' And he released her chin but to cup her face with both hands. 'Shall I show you?'

And he bent his head and started to kiss her.

She wrenched her head back. 'I'll scream the place down!'

'I doubt if anyone would hear over the band, but go ahead if it makes you feel you've shown a token resistance.'

'What?'

The fingers of one hand travelled down the side of her neck and ran along the bodice of her dress, across the tops of her breasts, so that she trembled involuntarily and he felt it through his fingers. 'I mean it's all an act, isn't it, Vivian? This stop-start approach of yours.' His blue eyes were supremely mocking now.

'Is that why you think I took up with Ralph?' she asked out of a dry throat.

'I have no idea, nor do I care to be enlightened,' he drawled, 'but we have some unfinished business.' And he drew her into his arms. 'Scream away now, Vivian,' he invited. 'It'll be too late in a moment.'

'Could...could I just talk some sense instead?' she pleaded. 'Things haven't come out right, you see—'

'I'm surprised they ever do with you,' he murmured.

She sagged against him suddenly, not in deference to his physical dominance or in acknowledgment that even now she wasn't immune to having her senses ignited by him, but because it had all gone so horribly wrong and, to use his words, once again she was a walking disaster.

And when he began to kiss her she didn't resist, she didn't have the will or the strength left, but she didn't respond either. In fact, to her horror, she started to cry.

He lifted his head. 'Oh, come now,' he said scornfully. 'Whatever else I like to think about you, Vivian, surely you've got more spirit than that.'

But she buried her head in his shoulder and sobbed bitterly, then pulled herself out of his arms and sat down on the bed again, almost doubled over as she held herself and rocked backwards and forwards, desperately trying to overcome these weak, ridiculous tears.

'You'll give yourself hiccups,' he warned.

She took no notice, then felt him sit down beside her and prise one of her hands free and put a glass into it. It was his drink, she saw, and he guided it to her lips. It was liqueur brandy and it did the trick. So that in a few minutes, although racked by the odd shudder, she was dry-eyed and able to say, 'Thanks. I think this has all got a bit much for me. Sorry.'

'Would you like to—talk sense now?' he said slowly, looking down at her with a frown.

'No.' She sniffed and swallowed some more brandy.

'Well, don't blame Ralph; it was all my idea. Um…how does one get away from here? Because I think I need to.' She looked up at him at last.

The frown was still in his eyes as they rested on her tear-streaked face, the blotches on her throat, the way her hands were clenched around the stem of the balloon glass resting in her pink silk lap. And it came to him that whatever she was, Vivian Florey, even when her eyes showed him she was scared of him, she never backed away… Whatever designs she had, whatever plan she'd concocted tonight to get Clover Wines, whatever disasters seemed to follow her around, there was something unusually gallant and brave about her.

He took the glass out of her hands and put it on the floor and lay back with her in his arms. She made a husky little sound of surprise, but he stilled it with his finger on her lips and just held her against him. Then he moved them up the bed to a more comfortable position, but still he only held her.

And they lay together until the shudders and tremors her tears had brought to her subsided completely and she was warm and soft in his arms, and, he hoped, feeling safe for the moment from the turmoil he himself, he had to admit, had helped to create in her life. Why he should feel like this about a girl who had undoubtedly been single-minded in her pursuit of commercial gain, who'd made a fool of him with his own brother, who had kissed him wholeheartedly a couple of times yet pulled back from the brink only hours ago, he wasn't sure.

But one thing he was sure of: he might never get her out of his system unless he did this. Or was it even simpler? He couldn't let her go without obliterating Ralph from her mind? The thought caused him to grimace but didn't stop him, because nothing could now, he knew…

He stroked her hair and kissed the soft hollow at the base of her throat.

Vivian stirred and looked at him with a mixture of wariness and surprise. But he stilled the wariness by kissing her eyelids and holding her gently. And he used every ounce of restraint he possessed to bring her alive beneath his hands and his mouth.

If she'd ever understood the kind of siege she was under during it, Vivian was to think in the days to come, she still would have had little chance of withstanding it. Weary and emotional, filled with a bleak sense of disaster, aching with his earlier rejection, as she probably would for the rest of her life, but above all still having that intrinsic sense of safety with Lleyton Dexter, despite the things he'd said, she was doomed almost from the start.

She simply had no answer for the things he did and the way he did them. She wasn't proof against being stroked and warmed and filled with delight as he made his acquaintance with her body slowly, delicately, and then more and more intimately. She could only quiver helplessly as her dress was unzipped and he helped her out of it, revealing a pair of shell-pink lacy briefs, a tiny, frilly suspender belt and sheer nylons. No bra, because the dress had one built in.

She had no sense of nakedness as he held her close again and buried his head in her hair, instead a sense of rightness at being able to press her body against his, a sense of just the two of them alone on the planet and a feeling of joy in her bruised heart. Why? she wondered. Because this wasn't, couldn't be an angry reprisal for what she'd done? Not this lovely, slow path he was leading her along, not this mutual sense of need and give and take. And she could feel the need in him, but also the restraint, the way he was committing himself to her pleasure and succeeding beyond all her expectations.

By the time he shed his clothes she was driven to a dreamy nirvana, unable to bear a separation from him, dying to welcome him back into her embrace, dying to be made feel so light and smooth and special again, as if she'd been made specially for Lleyton Dexter, in fact, made to fit, made to order. As if her femininity was the exact counterpart for his masculinity, as if her feminine psyche, the true heart of it, had never been released before and only he could do it.

Then, gradually, he increased the tempo as he made her aware of every part of her body and how he could make it sensitive and sensuous. The nape of her neck, the path between her breasts, the curve of her hips, the soft skin of her inner thighs. And he did things that sometimes made her stop and gasp and look at him wide-eyed, telling him she'd never experienced them before and wasn't sure about them, but each time his blue eyes seemed to say—Trust me, Vivian and she did.

Until she became more and more confident, more and more a partner in every way, able to dispense her own magic with her hands and lips on his body. And finally to be claimed, welcoming if not dying of need and desire, and be spun away into a pleasure dome of perfect sensation. Something that had never happened to her before, she realised, as she clung to him and felt his own reaction shudder through his body.

She couldn't talk for an age, and neither did he. She could no more have been parted from him in the aftermath than she could have flown to the moon. She felt as if she never wanted to be parted from him because it was as if she'd given him her soul. She felt as if she understood at last what true intimacy between a man and a woman was, and there was nothing she ever could or would want to hide from Lleyton Dexter because he knew her now, body and soul.

And she could never be the same with anyone else.

But as their breathing steadied at last, and he smoothed her hair and smiled into her eyes, someone knocked on the door.

She tensed, they both tensed, then a voice came through the panels. A voice that said, 'Vivi, let me in—it's Ralph.'

She saw the shutter come down in Lleyton's eyes and the hard line his mouth set in; she felt the suddenly cruel pressure of his arms around her. And she read the plain, grim warning in his eyes. A warning to stay silent.

She did, as she would have anyway, and Ralph knocked again twice before they heard footsteps retreating.

Then Lleyton released her and got up in one swift, fluid movement.

She sat up, running her fingers through her hair, and opened her mouth to speak, but he got in first.

'I'm sorry if I pipped Ralph to the post.' He pulled on his trousers and reached for his shirt. 'But you should have warned me.'

Vivian felt the colour drain from her face and she reached for the sheet to draw it up around her. 'You didn't. He…I had no idea—'

'Vivi.' Lleyton glanced at her with supreme irony and sat on the side of the bed to pull his socks on. 'Spare me convoluted not to mention untruthful explanations. If you thought I didn't like the idea of Ralph ducking under my guard in any respect, you were right. If *that* was the plan, it succeeded—'

'I don't know what you mean!' Vivian broke in, her eyes dazed with incomprehension.

'Then I'll spell it out for you,' he said roughly. 'The

way this happened tonight takes the responsibility for it away from you and places it squarely with me. That's why you so delicately disengaged yourself this afternoon, isn't it? Because you were coming across a little too willingly.'

'No. That doesn't make sense—I wasn't exactly unwilling a little while ago,' she whispered.

'After threatening to scream then indulging in a storm of tears, no,' he said sardonically. 'You even got me to think that you were quite…gallant. But it still all adds up to one thing—you wanted me in the position of perpetrator, instigator, or whatever the hell, not *you*, and there was no better way than to use Ralph to—rev me up and get me to the point where you had little choice tonight, Vivian.'

Her lips parted and her eyes were huge.

He smiled coldly—so coldly her heart seemed to freeze. 'Don't tell me you don't know enough about men to know that?'

She licked her suddenly dry lips. 'But why would I…?'

'Why? So you could still hold on to, or *appear*,' he said scathingly, 'to hold on to your frequently made claim that you wouldn't sleep with me to get anything.'

Vivian could only stare at him again, absolutely stunned.

'Which is not to say you don't also fancy Ralph,' he continued. 'But it should have crossed your mind that you don't get anything for nothing—and that was Ralph, coming to claim his pay-off.' He reached for his shoes.

'No! Look—'

'You didn't *use* him tonight, then? And appear to enjoy every minute of it?'

'No. Well, yes, but…' She stopped helplessly and watched the long line of his back beneath the white dress shirt as he tied his shoelaces, watched the play of his muscles beneath the thin cotton and shivered.

Then he stood up. 'So now you've got both the Dexter brothers in tow,' he drawled. 'Believe me, Vivian, that's quite an achievement, but this one is about to back out of the game.' And he leant down leisurely and pulled the sheet from her grasp.

She gasped.

'Just taking a last look at a girl who almost fooled me.' And that damning blue gaze travelled slowly down her body, taking in every curve that he now knew so well, every soft, sensitive spot where, with the lightest touch, he had caused her to arch against him in dizzy delight.

'Oh, yes,' he said softly, his gaze coming back to hers, more scorching and contemptuous than she'd ever seen it, 'very lovely, but you're a consummate actress, Vivian Florey. I'm beginning to wonder whether your fears of flying, heights and lifts aren't all an invention too, but I'll give you this—you did earn Clover Wines in the end. On your back.' He dropped the sheet, found his jacket and tie and walked out the verandah way.

CHAPTER SEVEN

'MRS DEXTER? It's Vivian Florey—please could you let me in, I need to talk to you?'

It was a bare half-hour later, and as Ralph had tapped on her door earlier, she was now tapping on his mother's. The ball was still going—although a tiptoe reconnaissance around the upstairs verandah had shown Vivian that the numbers had reduced a bit and a line of light showed under Amelia's door.

She tapped again and the door opened abruptly. Amelia Dexter was minus her make-up and wearing a navy and white spotted robe over her nightgown, but she was still an autocratic figure. 'Vivian,' she said, her expression rigid with distaste, 'you're the last person I want to talk to, and especially at this time of night. Go to bed!'

'No, please don't slam the door on me,' Vivian begged. 'I really need to make someone understand and…and I need help.'

Amelia hesitated and frowned, taking in Vivian's pale face, the jeans she wore with a cream jumper and her obvious agitation. She clicked her tongue. 'To be honest I would have thought you'd caused enough drama one way or another, but come in. I must warn you this had better be good, however!'

And she swirled away from the door, leaving Vivian to enter and close it. It was a huge bedroom, with a chintz-covered lounge suite in front of a fireplace at one end. There was a silver tea tray on the coffee table but only one cup, as yet unused, and a plate of macaroons. Amelia, it would appear, had been just about to sit down to a nightcap.

Vivian swallowed, and would have given anything for a cup of tea. But she wasn't offered one as Amelia poured for herself and sat back with her cup.

'So? How *could* you?' Lleyton's mother said. 'I don't know what your game is—'

'Mrs Dexter,' Vivian broke in, 'may I just explain things first? You'll probably still hate me, but—it's not altogether as you think.' And, taking a deep breath, she told Amelia Dexter the whole story, with only two omissions—one of them being the exact details of what had taken place between her and Lleyton so recently.

When she'd finished, Amelia opened and closed her mouth several times, to finally say, 'Well, it does explain some things, but—' she looked at Vivian a little helplessly '—how do I know if it's all true?'

Vivian produced the grey velvet box. 'Please give this back to Lleyton. It's the ring. I wasn't going to wear it, but that's another story. And Ralph will be able to tell you, if he's honest about it, why we did what we did. I don't know why he came knocking at my door tonight,' she said evenly, 'but I made it quite plain to him that there couldn't be anything between us. I also made it plain he shouldn't be interfering between Lleyton and Ginny, even with her connivance, and that this was an opportunity to get out of that role, for *both* of us to get out our assumed roles, and perhaps bring them together.'

'Ginny,' Amelia said slowly, and sighed. 'Well, I imagine she had her reasons. And Ralph and Lleyton have always…needled each other.'

'I know. I just wish I'd stopped to think, but it didn't occur to me that the animosity they feel towards each other could be activated over me. I don't really think it has been...' Vivian paused. 'At least, I hope it hasn't, and I just had to tell *someone* the truth because I've always felt guilty about marring Mag's special week. But I really had no idea what I was precipitating when I came here.'

Amelia watched her closely for a full minute.

Vivian had showered and her hair was damp, there were blue shadows beneath her eyes, her face was still pale and her expression was haunted.

'I see,' Lleyton's mother said at last. She got up, walked into the bathroom and returned with her cup rinsed out. Then she poured Vivian a cup of tea from the silver pot.

'Thanks,' Vivian said gratefully.

'There's one thing I'm still not too sure about,' Amelia said slowly. 'Was it Lleyton himself or the wine account that kept you here at Harvest Moon when you did begin to understand—things?'

Vivian looked away. 'There was a misunderstanding about that too,' she said awkwardly. 'But I can't blame him for thinking I was...well, on the make personally as well as business-wise, and that we might...have a short-term relationship. It wouldn't suit me, though.'

'So you didn't fall in love with him, Vivian?'

It was the question she'd been dreading and hoping to be able to avoid. But there was no avoiding Amelia's dark blue gaze that was so like her son's. She swallowed a mouthful of tea. 'I thought I might, but, no, I didn't. The other thing I wanted to ask you to do is tell Lleyton I couldn't accept the wine account now, or the shampoo, so Goodman's will take Clover off their books altogether.'

'Why don't you tell him all this yourself?'

'I don't want to have to see Lleyton again. I...it's impossible to explain things to him, and anyway now's the time to...just do it. That's the other thing. *Please*, how can I leave this place? Now,' Vivian said urgently. 'Really, I've had enough and I'm all packed. Would it be possible to ring for a taxi?' She clenched her hands so that her knuckles showed white.

Amelia shook her head slowly. 'No, we're too far away from anywhere. But I could organise something, I suppose. My dear, why don't you wait in your room for a little while? Our head gardener doubles as my chauffeur; I'll see if I can raise him.'

'Couldn't I wait here?' Vivian asked nervously.

Amelia looked at her sharply. 'You're not...scared of Lleyton, are you?'

Vivian closed her eyes and wondered how to tell his mother that she couldn't endure another encounter with her son. She licked her lips. 'No, of course not. But...' She trailed off uncertainly.

'All right,' Amelia said abruptly. 'Sit tight.' And she left the room.

Twenty minutes later she walked down the staircase with Vivian and led her out to a dark blue Range Rover, waiting outside the front door with its lights on, its engine running.

'Your luggage is in, Vivian, and I hope you'll forgive me, but this seems the best way to go.'

'Oh, once I get to a train station or something I can take care of myself, Mrs Dexter,' Vivian assured her. 'Thank you for helping me.'

'Yes, well.' Amelia shrugged, and to Vivian's surprise, hugged her. 'In you get—and take care.'

Vivian climbed up the high step and said, 'Hello! Sorry about this—' And stopped as if she'd been shot. Because it was no stranger at the wheel, no anonymous head gardener dressed in jeans and a navy windcheater. It was Lleyton.

And as Amelia closed the door on Vivian, he slid in the clutch and drove off.

'Of all the—how could she?' Vivian said despairingly. 'You told me your mother was a pillar of respectability!'

'She is. Do up your seat belt,' he advised dryly. 'In fact, if she hadn't bumped into me while she was looking for Richards you might have got away with it.'

'Got away with what? You make me sound like a criminal trying to pull off some kind of heist—where are we going?' she added tautly.

'Anywhere to get away from this madhouse. Where, as a matter of interest, would *you* like to go, Vivian?'

'Civilisation, where there are trains and taxis and buses and planes so I can get myself home!' She fumbled for her seat belt at last as they drove through an impressive set of gates, which she'd never seen before, and Lleyton put his foot down. 'Are you all right to drive?' she asked with sudden anxiety.

'What do you mean?' He turned his head, but it was too dark to decipher his expression, although his tone of his voice had been roughly impatient.

'You were drinking very strong brandy not that long ago!'

'Actually, you drank as much of it as I did. Do you think that accounts for it?'

She didn't pretend to misunderstand, but she didn't respond.

'Vivian?'

'I don't want to talk about it, Lleyton. It's over. You made your judgement—well, I've made mine now.'

'My mother tells me I may have misjudged you.'

'Whatever,' Vivian said wearily. 'It doesn't alter the basics. It doesn't mean anything, really.' She gestured helplessly. 'It's over now and the last thing I want to do is talk about it.'

'She didn't go into any details,' he said. 'She told me I should just listen to you. But something you imparted to her must have won her over.'

Vivian laid her head back and refused to speak.

'More lies, Vivian?' he suggested. 'Is that why you were desperate to get away without having to face me?'

She didn't lift her head, but she turned it to watch the night flying past her window. 'I did tell her a lie, yes.'

'I wondered about that.'

'Did you? It must be nice to have me so well figured out, Lleyton.'

'Vivian.' His voice was grim now. 'If you've got anything to say, say it.'

'OK—how far is it to the nearest station?'

He put his foot down again and Vivian clutched at the armrest, but she stubbornly refused to give way to his intimidation, as she thought of it, or to let him see how upset she was. In fact she curled up away from him and, after a few more miles, fell asleep.

Dawn was just breaking as he drew up in front of Sydney's Mascot Airport.

Vivian blinked, stretched, and looked around her dazedly. Then she turned to him with her lips parted, and it all came back to her: the awful nightmare of her last night at Harvest Moon. 'Is this…? This is the airport,' she stammered. 'Look, I didn't expect you to bring me all this way. I could have got a train or something.'

Lleyton rested one elbow on the steering wheel and looked her over thoroughly. 'Before the crack of dawn? Maybe not. Is this where you want to be, though?' He was clipped and curt, and something about the way he was looking her over made her conscious of what a mess she was.

She rubbed her face and tried to comb her hair with her fingers. 'Well, yes!' she assured him confusedly. 'It couldn't be a better place to start going home. Um...'

'Then hop out. I'll get your luggage.' He got out himself.

But when her luggage was on the pavement and she was desperately thinking of something to say, he said, 'Wait here. I'll park the car. At this time of day it'll only take me a couple of minutes. Don't go anywhere, Vivian,' he ordered.

She swallowed—and sat down on her suitcase. As he'd promised, he was back within minutes.

'You don't have to stay. I can—' she began to say, but he ignored her and started to wheel her suitcase into the concourse. Within not many minutes more he had her booked first class onto the first flight for Brisbane, leaving in an hour. Then he steered her to an exclusive lounge and suggested she might like to use the powder room.

She escaped thankfully and made some running repairs to herself, washing her face, dealing with her hair, but mostly trying to get her mind into some kind of order. When she came back he had ordered coffee and pastries and was sitting waiting for her.

She sighed as she sat down opposite a steaming cup and inhaled the aroma. She said gruffly, 'Thanks. Do I ever need this. But you didn't have to—'

'Vivian, if you say that once more I'm liable to throttle you.'

She picked up her cup and looked at him over the rim. Whatever toll the night had taken of her—and the mirror in the powder room had told its own tale: smudges like bruises beneath her eyes, an unnatural pallor—how she wished she had some make-up!—and a decidedly limp bearing that she didn't seem to be able to correct—he was not showing the same signs, apart from obviously not having shaved.

He looked disturbingly big, alive, in command of himself and everything else, she thought with a tinge of bitterness, although not in the best of moods.

She put the cup down and rubbed her forehead with her fingertips. 'Two things, Lleyton. Your mother has the ring and I don't want Clover at all. We—Goodman's, I mean—will get along without it.'

'Because of what I said?'

'Because I should never have entered into that kind of deal with you in the first place,' she refuted steadily, although with enormous inward effort to keep her voice and her eyes steady. 'Because I now find myself morally opposed to accepting anything from you, Lleyton, or being—bought.'

He looked at his watch. 'Vivian, four hours ago you were in my arms making love to me as if…as if it had never happened that way for you before.'

She shrugged and picked up her cup again to sip her coffee.

'You don't want to talk about it?'

Every nerve within her screamed at her to tell him that *he* was the one who had flung everything about their love-making back at her. But she knew she would never allow herself to trust Lleyton Dexter again—so what point was there in trying to sort through the tangled explanations of the night—Ralph, Ginny Deacon—let alone her own feelings?

'No,' she said at last.

'What about any consequences?' he said grimly.

She closed her eyes. 'I doubt if it could happen to you twice, Lleyton, and mathematically it's highly unlikely.'

'Do you mean on the scale of averages as in two women, you and Ginny, or the time of the month?' he asked sardonically.

She swallowed. 'The time of the month.'

He was silent for a long moment, but she got the feeling his gaze was looking through to her soul. Then he said, 'And there's nothing you'd like to add, Miss Florey?'

'I'm not in a witness box, Lleyton—is there anything *you'd* like to add?' A spark of anger lit her eyes at last.

He sat back, but before he could say anything she went on, 'As a matter of fact there is something I'd like to add. If you can't get Ginny Deacon out of your heart, stop torturing yourself and her.'

A soft twin bell tone sounded and her flight was announced. Vivian's eyes widened as it suddenly came home to her what she was about to do shortly—fly. 'Oh, no,' she said dismally. 'This is the last thing I need right now.'

'You assured me it was what you wanted,' he said dryly.

'It is, but I haven't had time to prepare myself.'

'There's still about twenty minutes before take-off,' he said, and watched her narrowly.

Her shoulders slumped.

'Why don't you remember how brave you were with me?' he suggested.

'That's the last thing I want to—' She broke off and bit her lip. 'Uh…perhaps you're right. If I can do that, this should be a breeze. Yes.' She stood up with determination stamped into every line of her figure and reached for her purse. 'OK, you really don't need to come any further, Lleyton. I know which gate it is, so…let's make it goodbye now. I'm sorry it all turned out to be such a fiasco, but at least you can go back to Harvest Moon and help Mag enjoy her wedding week.'

He stood up. 'I'll walk you to the gate, Vivian.'

'That's only prolonging the—' Again she broke off.

'The agony?' he murmured, and waited, watching her like a hawk.

She looked away. 'Not at all. I just…I don't need my hand held!'

'All right,' he said, suddenly amiable, 'I won't do that, but I intend to see you onto this plane.'

'Don't worry,' she flashed at him, 'I'm not about to give you the slip and turn up at Harvest Moon again to take up where I left off—is that what you're worried about?'

'Not at all,' he drawled. 'After you, Vivian.'

She marched out of the lounge with her head held high. He followed and walked beside her in silence until they came to the gate lounge. Then she stopped, looked out of the huge glass window at the plane, swallowed, and patted her jeans pockets and started to search through her purse for her ticket and boarding pass a little frantically.

'Here.' He took her purse from her and reached into the outside pocket to produce both items. Then he put his arms around her.

'Lleyton,' she whispered, her eyes wide and wary as all sorts of memories of the things this man had done to her came tumbling back into her mind.

He studied the dew of sweat on her brow, and she felt him sigh. 'Vivian, you can do this. And you were…very lovely to make love to. I'm sorry if I indicated otherwise. Is there anything you'd like to tell me?'

Her lips parted and her soul cried out to her to be honest with him. But just as Stan Goodman's face had used to swim into her mind, Ginny Deacon's did now, and not only that but the sheer frightening vacuum he'd left her in only five hours ago, naked, exposed and once again rejected, so that she still didn't know how she was going to cope with it…

'No,' she said very quietly. 'Goodbye, Lleyton, I'll be fine.' And she freed herself and walked away. She didn't look back once.

But as she sat, trembling inwardly as much from her emotions as her fear of flying, in her first-class seat, she was to discover that the good side of Lleyton Dexter, the side she hadn't been able to stop herself from trusting, was still with her. Just before take-off, the stewardess who'd been at the gate slid into the empty seat beside her.

'I believe you're a bit nervous,' she said, and put her hand over Vivian's on the armrest. 'Don't be. I've done this so many times.'

'How did you know…?' Vivian stared at her.

'The man you were with told me. And it always helps to have someone to chat to—you have the most beautiful curly hair, by the way!'

It was hard to believe it was only four days since she'd left her apartment when she walked back into it and stood looking around.

And she found herself musing that it was no wonder the past four days had a dreamlike quality to them. So much had happened in such a short time, and really, she reflected, how could one fall in love with a man in four days?

She closed her eyes and felt herself sway from sheer exhaustion. There seemed to be only one thing to do and that was to crawl into bed, although it was late morning. Which she did—but for nearly an hour, instead of falling asleep, it all kept going round in her mind: what she'd done, what she should have done, what she shouldn't have done…

What was taking place at Harvest Moon right at this moment? What explanations had been made for her moonlight flit? Had Amelia passed her confidences on to Lleyton, and if so what difference would it make?

None, probably, she answered herself, unless Ralph chose to come clean. Because it not only sounded so far-fetched but she'd played her part too well; she'd even laid the groundwork for it herself when, not that far away at the Riverside restaurant, she'd taunted Lleyton about her preferences in men without ever dreaming he had a brother who could fit the bill perfectly.

Had it been supremely naïve to think that Ralph wouldn't disregard her warning and would try to make something out of nothing between them? Obviously, she thought dejectedly. Why else would he have come knocking at her door at that time of night?

But perhaps her biggest single error had been to continue with the farce for so long in the name of Goodman's. And that, as it happened, was the only thing she could rectify…

The sun was setting when she woke, having fallen asleep without realising it. She got up and showered and made herself a snack, then went to sit at a writing table beside her answering machine, which was blinking madly.

All the messages were social bar one, the last one, which had been left just before she'd arrived home that morning. And she stared at the machine, stunned, as Stan Goodman's personal assistant relayed the news that Stan had had a mild heart attack two days ago but the news from Lleyton Dexter himself this morning, that

Goodman's had secured the Clover wine and shampoo accounts, had buoyed him up considerably.

'What?' she whispered. 'Oh, no!'

'Does he know about Stan's heart attack?'

It was eight-thirty the next morning and Vivian was in her office. She had been in the office for over an hour, pacing around like a caged lion waiting for Stan's assistant.

She'd spoken to Stan's wife, Isabelle, the night before, and got the news that he was in hospital but would be released today, although he'd have to take things easy for a while. Isabelle Goodman had gone on to say that Stan had been immeasurably relieved by the news of the Clover accounts and had asked her to thank Vivian from the bottom of his dicky heart. He'd also asked her to tell Vivian that he had every faith in her coming up with a brilliant campaign for Clover wines.

'No,' Lucy White, Stan's PA, said now, with a grimace. 'I didn't tell him about Stan's health because—well, I just didn't want to do anything to jeopardise the deal! It's about the only thing that's going to save us, and anyway, you're the vital one, not Stan.'

Vivian sat down heavily behind her desk. 'So what did he say? What exactly did he say? Lleyton Dexter.'

Lucy White, fifty and a professional businesswoman but also a motherly person, looked at Vivian with a frown. 'Is there some problem, Vivi?'

Vivian shook her head after a moment. 'I'd just like to know. I…he…I left not knowing it was in the bag, so to speak.' It was obvious that Lucy was unaware of the deal Vivian had undertaken to secure the Clover accounts.

Lucy's expression cleared. 'He said, when I told him Stan was unavailable, that it didn't matter, I could pass it on to you that he was most impressed with the labels you'd designed. And he gave me the name of someone for us to contact in their contracts department, as well as someone to liase with about their different wines, et cetera. All our copy should be channelled through this person for approval, apparently. He himself won't be available for quite a while, he said. Vivi,' she went on excitedly, 'this is big! Not only labels but magazine advertising, as well as eventually television. You're a very clever girl!'

And if ever a girl was caught in a Catch 22 situation, she was, Vivian thought miserably. What on earth was she going to do? Weigh up her loyalty to Stan, who'd been like a father to her at times and had certainly promoted her career, against compromising her morals?

But wasn't that being overly dramatic and overstating the case? From her point of view, perhaps. From Lleyton's... Why would he have done it unless it was some kind of a test—another one? Out of the goodness of his heart, even although he believed she'd duped him, provoked him and tried to get off with his brother?

Perhaps his mother had made him listen, she thought. But if he'd told Lucy to pass on to her that he wasn't going to be available for quite a while, wasn't that akin to telling her he was off-limits now? Which had to mean nothing his mother had told him had made any difference, either because he hadn't believed it or because...he'd always meant it when he'd said he wasn't for her, even after he'd slept with her.

So, it had to be a reward for going to bed with him, and whether it had been awarded with malice, to make her feel...bought, so he could say he'd kept his part of the deal, or because he regretted what had happened, in any event, every instinct she possessed told her to refuse it—because to be beholden in any way to him was unthinkable.

She licked her lips and realised that Lucy had departed, obviously thinking that Vivian was concentrating on ideas, and that a cup of tea had been brought for her without her realizing it.

She pulled it towards her, then dropped her face in her hands and breathed very deeply—because she was starting to feel nauseous, as she often did in times of crisis.

The more she thought about it, the more she saw that she was in a cleft stick. She couldn't abandon Stan Goodman in his hour of need, she couldn't put him through the trauma of telling him she refused to work on the Clover account. And she couldn't excise Lleyton Dexter out of her life and her heart as she'd planned to do by having Goodman's reject Clover.

She couldn't even, she realised, use Stan's illness as any form of an excuse to Lleyton for going back on her word, simply because it went against the grain with her to trade in excuses.

'And if he thinks,' she murmured to herself, 'I slept my way to getting Clover, let him think it.' She leant back and closed her eyes and wondered sadly what choice she'd had two nights ago. Because the more she thought of it the more she realized she'd been at the mercy of a most dangerously attractive man. And whether he'd been motivated by a desire to outdo Ralph or to get something in return for giving her Clover, whatever, she had no answer for the way he'd made her feel.

'So you live and learn, even when you think you know it all,' she whispered aloud. 'Let it be a lesson, Vivian Florey…'

* * *

'Vivi—these are brilliant!' Stan Goodman said to her three weeks later.

It was his first day back in the office. Isabelle had taken him away for a holiday and barred him from all business so that now he was looking tanned, fit and relaxed.

But he frowned suddenly and looked at Vivian closely. 'You OK?'

'Fine! Well, I've been working really hard on Clover—you know how it is when you get inspired and it's hard to knock off,' she said humorously.

'I've never seen you looking so thin and pale before, though,' he said slowly. 'What exactly did happen with Lleyton Dexter?'

Vivian waved a hand airily. 'I didn't get to go to the wedding. We resolved it before then. Actually, it got a bit complicated. His family ganged up on him and had his ex-wife at Harvest Moon in a bid to bring about a reconciliation. I'm afraid I had to draw the line at… Well—' she shrugged '—being a decoy against a nameless bunch of women is rather different from an ex-wife who is still in love with him.'

'I didn't know that!' Stan looked surprised.

'That he was married once? Neither did I.' Vivian raised her eyebrows expressively. 'I actually fell into the Hawkesbury River when I found out. So—' she chuckled '—things were a little confused. But I got it, Stan. Do you really think they're OK?' She gestured at the layouts on his desk.

'Brilliant. I love the Latino influence you've used—I know it's an Australian wine, but I think a cosmopolitan flavour gives it a breadth and a depth, especially since it's going into the export market and also here at home. Did you model this guy on anyone?'

Vivian glanced down at a shadowy look-alike Ralph,

and wondered if Stan could have any conception of how she'd agonised over using that look in the light of subsequent events, despite Lleyton's original approval. But, having got that idea in her mind when she'd first started to think about promoting wine, it had been almost impossible to shake, and in the end she'd told herself he wouldn't be so petty as to object now. Nothing else she'd come up with had had the same feeling anyway.

But she wasn't completely sure that he wouldn't take it as an affront, and it had added to the inner turmoil that saw her losing her breakfast on a fairly regular basis.

She said uneasily to Stan, 'I also did these, just in case—well, to have a back-up.'

Stan studied her offerings, then said decisively, 'No. I think you've hit the jackpot with the first lot, Vivi. We'll go with them. OK, we'll scan them and send them down for approval. And I think you need a break, my dear.'

'There's a long weekend coming up this weekend, Stan. I may take an extra day and go…fishing,' she said with a grin. 'By the way, it's wonderful to see you looking so well!'

'Vivi—I have to thank you for a lot of it, and I do, from the bottom of my heart.'

Which almost made it worthwhile, Vivian reflected several times over the next few days, as the whole agency waited with bated breath for Clover's approval of the wine presentation.

But nothing had come through by the Friday morning before the long weekend, and once again Vivian's nerves were stretched to breaking point. And once again she lost her breakfast just after getting to work.

She had to stop this, she reflected as she washed her face and leant her forehead against the mirror in the bathroom attached to her office. She'd be twenty-six in two days' time; surely she should have better control of her nerves by now?

She dried her hands, then paused as she heard her phone ring. But her secretary, who was young and eager and in her first job, must have rushed to answer it because Vivian heard her say, 'I'm so sorry but Miss Florey isn't available at the moment. She's not feeling very well, but she always comes good by about ten o'clock. May I get her to call you back?'

Vivian rushed out, but Linda Goodhew was putting the phone down.

'Linda, you'll have people thinking I'm pregnant—I'm fine, all you had to do was call me! Who was it?'

'Some woman, but she didn't give her name, just said she'd call back. Are you sure you're fine? You don't look it,' Linda said concernedly. 'And the same thing happened a few days ago. Why don't you go and see a doctor?'

'I...I will. Just don't spread the word around the whole world. Sorry,' Vivian said contritely as Linda looked downcast, 'but it's nothing serious.'

'If you say so.'

'I do. OK, let's get to work. I've got some letters to get out.'

By five-thirty no word had come from Clover, so Vivian went home, convinced she'd lost the agency the accounts with her look-alike Ralph.

It was a hot, steamy evening, so she showered and changed into her black happy shirt and assembled a meal of cold meat and salad that she didn't feel like eating. She had no plans for the long weekend, and knew she wouldn't be taking any extra days off until the sheer torture of not knowing about Clover was ended.

Then her buzzer sounded, and when she switched on the security screen it was Lleyton.

'You!' she gasped down the intercom. 'What—'

'Just let me in, Vivian,' he ordered.

'But—'

'I won't go away,' he threatened. 'So if you'd rather I made a scene, or if you're too much of a coward to see me—'

'I'm not!'

'Then let me in, Vivian.'

She clenched her teeth and punched the button. Then she looked down at herself and raced into her bedroom to strip off her happy shirt and pull on a pair of white shorts and a yellow blouse. She was still buttoning up the blouse as her doorbell rang, and had no shoes on. But before she could find a pair it rang again, and kept ringing.

She abandoned her search for shoes and marched to open it in her bare feet.

'Who do you think you are, Lleyton Dexter?' she said militantly.

His gaze drifted down her and rested on her bare feet. He was formally dressed in the same grey suit he'd worn the last time he'd been in Brisbane with her, with a pale blue shirt and a navy tie and he carried a suit bag. Very much the powerful tycoon.

He said, 'History repeats itself, Vivian. No shoes, I see. I hope I didn't get you out of bed—or interrupt anything?' That blue gaze travelled upwards and rested on her blouse.

She looked downwards and cursed herself inwardly because it was buttoned up crookedly. 'No, but—'

'As to who I am.' Their gazes clashed at last as he broke in on what she'd been about to say, and she flinched at the sheer anger and mockery in his eyes. 'The father of your child, by any chance?'

CHAPTER EIGHT

VIVIAN'S mouth dropped open.

'Don't tell me it hadn't occurred to you?' he murmured, and stepped over the threshold, closing the door. He dumped the bag he was carrying onto the floor.

She backed a couple of steps, and tripped. He put out a hand and caught her wrist, saving her from falling. Then he stood towering over her, taking in every last detail of her, until finally he said scathingly, 'Only you could be so dumb, Vivian. Morning sickness, looking pale and thin—'

'Who...who told you I had morning sickness?' she whispered incredulously.

'Your secretary as good as told Mrs Harper when she tried to get hold of you for me this morning. But I only have to look at you to know something's happened, and I can't think of anything else that would fit the bill so well.'

Vivian opened her mouth, but no words would come. She was shocked enough to be unresisting as he led her into the lounge and told her to sit down. She sank onto a lemon settee and watched with wide, disbelieving eyes as he stripped off his jacket and pulled off his tie. Then he reached into an inner jacket pocket and pulled out some folded sheets of paper.

'So,' he said grimly. 'You decided to persevere with Ralph.' He threw the sheets down on the coffee table in front of her.

She glanced at her own artwork and flinched. 'Lleyton,'

she said huskily, 'this was an idea you approved of before I even knew Ralph *existed*.'

'And you were the one, Vivian, who assured me you wouldn't be touching any Clover accounts with a barge-pole because you couldn't be bought,' he shot at her. 'Then this.' He gestured towards the sheets.

'You were the one who made sure I couldn't refuse them,' she cried. 'I mean, you actually gave them to Goodman's without telling me!'

'You could have backed out. You could have told your boss what had happened and why you felt morally opposed to the whole deal,' he taunted.

'No, I—' She stopped and tried to gather herself, but she was still reeling inwardly from so many shocks it was impossible. She closed her eyes and said tonelessly, 'What difference does it make?'

'I'll tell you, Vivian.' He sat down opposite. 'You'd have felt much more comfortable as my wife had you maintained the moral high ground and had you not chosen to flaunt—to *continue* to flaunt Ralph at me.'

Her head started to spin, she went as pale as paper, and the world started to recede from her.

Although she didn't actually faint, it was only his prompt action that saved her from it. He was up in a flash to sit down beside her, and he pushed her head gently down to her knees until she protested feebly. 'I'm f-fine now,' she stammered.

'Good,' he said unemotionally, and helped her to sit back. 'Would you happen to have any brandy?'

'Yes, but there's some mango-flavoured mineral water in the fridge. That would be...' she swallowed '...nicer.'

He raised an eyebrow for some reason, then went and got them a glass each. On the way back he passed her plate of cold meat and salad, and brought that over too.

'Does this happen often?' he queried. 'Have you been to a doctor yet?'

'No. And no. But—'

'So you haven't admitted to yourself that it's happened in spite of your mathematics?' He sat down beside her again.

She took a breath, accepted the glass and took a long swallow of mineral water, then took a piece of cheese and an olive from the salad on her plate and looked at him with a confused frown in her eyes. 'Surely after what happened with Ginny you wouldn't marry me because of…of…a baby?' She gestured.

'You don't think I'd allow an heir of mine to be brought up fatherless, Vivian? Especially by someone as prone to attracting disaster as you are?' His eyes were deep blue and supremely ironic.

Her lips parted and she nearly choked on a piece of cheese. 'That's…' She stopped and changed tack. 'Did you ever…did your mother ever…?' She couldn't go on.

'Tell me what you'd told her? Yes, she did. It was all a bit too far-fetched for me to believe. Especially when the Clover accounts didn't get thrown back in my face.'

'What about Ralph?' Vivian said after a long, uncomfortable pause.

He sat back with his arm along the back of the settee. 'Ralph gave me an explanation that did tally with what you told my mother, but he was so hangdog about it, especially when it came to knocking on your door at one-thirty in the morning—only to tell you, so he said, that he couldn't find *me* therefore the plan seemed to have failed. Would *you* have believed that, Vivian?'

'Yes,' she said bleakly. 'Well, it may have been a prelude to other things, but—'

'Other things?' Lleyton Dexter mused cynically.

'Not of my suggestion or to my liking, nor would he have found me willing,' she said definitely. 'And I don't care whether you believe me or not, Lleyton, because I'm certainly not going to marry you. There are several very good reasons for that!'

His lips twisted. 'Amazing what a sip of mineral water and a bit of cheese can do,' he marvelled.

'I've just started to get over the shock of you,' she retorted, and picked up a piece of ham and a bit of lettuce. 'OK, let's start at the top. I'll tell you why I had no choice but to take the Clover accounts, especially after you let it be known to Goodman's.' And she did so, precisely and unequivocally.

'I see,' he murmured, not visibly impressed or otherwise.

'So you may like to think you *bought* me,' she pressed on, 'but it wasn't the case. Stan has been like a father to me at times. Nor was I trying to...flaunt Ralph at you, but I couldn't for the life of me come up with anything half as good as these.' She gestured to the sheets lying on the table. 'I did do another presentation but Stan rejected it. This just happens to be a winner,' she said helplessly. 'I know it in my bones.'

'Go on.'

It took her a few moments to marshal her thoughts this time—for one thing it was curiously unnerving to be under his enigmatic scrutiny; it made her remember her blouse was still buttoned up crookedly and her feet were still bare. 'Well, I'm of the opinion you and Ginny will never get over each other, but that's neither here nor there,' she said, finishing rapidly, and could have kicked herself for bringing it up because it was tantamount to admitting she thought he didn't love *her*—something that should not be making the slightest difference.

'It is, as it happens,' he said.

She blinked at him.

'Here or there,' he supplied. 'But do continue, Vivian.'

She clenched her teeth. 'You must think I'm mad, Lleyton. You despise me, you think you can buy me, you suspect me of designs on your own brother, not to mention cheap strategies that I hate to even think about!'

'There was a certain—heat of the moment aspect to that,' he said sombrely.

'I'd hate to think what kind of insults you could devise if you really put your mind to it.' She shivered openly. 'But you yourself told me you wouldn't have the time to…to be married to anyone, let alone *me*, and now this! What kind of a marriage do you have in mind?' she asked with the utmost sarcasm.

He sat up. 'The best we can, Vivian, for a kid who was conceived in a moment of pleasure without any thought to the consequences. I lost the last one, I don't intend to lose this one by any of my own actions.'

'That's…that's crazy,' she whispered. 'That's as good as saying you would have stayed married to Ginny if…if…' She could only stare at him.

'Yes, I would have.'

'And you still don't reckon you love her?' she asked intensely.

'We seem to keep getting back to that. But—'

But Vivian had stood up, shaking and very pale again. 'Lleyton, this has gone on long enough,' she said jerkily. 'There is no baby.'

'You haven't—' He didn't finish, but she'd never seen him look harder or colder, and it seemed to spell out everything he thought of her.

'No! I was never pregnant!'

'So—how can you be so sure?'

She sat down again and rubbed her face incredulously. 'Do I have to give you a biology lesson?'

'Then why are sick in the mornings but come good around ten o'clock, and why are you looking like this?' he demanded harshly.

'I've been under a lot of strain and pressure. At work. What with Stan being sick and so on.' She glanced at him and read disbelief in his eyes and closed her own briefly. 'I told you once—heights, flying, *nausea* under pressure, lifts. That's all it was.'

'Hiccups—don't forget those,' he said.

She shrugged, and shot him a look of irony. 'That's about the only thing I haven't suffered from lately…' And couldn't believe it when she started to hiccup. 'Oh, no!'

He got up and walked into the kitchen. This time he came back with two glasses of brandy. 'I thought you were avoiding alcohol because you were pregnant…' He stopped.

She took a sip and breathed deeply, and the awful spectre of hysteria accompanied by painful hiccups receded as the warmth of the liquor slid down. 'I suppose that did sound suspicious, as well as what happened over the phone. I actually told my secretary she could be spreading rumours that I was pregnant, but I never for one moment thought—well, I didn't know it was you anyway. Why…why were you ringing me?'

'To take issue with you over these,' he said, and suddenly picked up the sheets of paper and crumpled them into a ball.

Vivian watched with her lips parted and her eyes wary.

'But…' He paused and looked down at her. 'If I read more into it than I should have—with Mrs Harper's help,' he conceded ruefully, 'it was because it made me think I had another chance.'

She blinked. 'What for? I don't understand.'

'Another chance with you, Vivian.'

She gasped. 'But...but there are so many things you...you hold against me. I've just run through them,' she said in a stronger voice, 'and that was damning enough, but it didn't include being a walking disaster! Lleyton, I can't believe this.'

He sat down beside her. 'Neither could I,' he said ironically. He shrugged. 'I walked away from you telling myself every last one of them. I wouldn't listen to my mother, or Ralph; I convinced myself it was over...' He stopped and sighed. 'But when I saw these—' he pointed to the screwed-up artwork '—I knew that it wasn't. I couldn't believe how...angry it made me. Then thinking you were pregnant made me angrier, but not because of the fact of it,' he said wearily.

'Why?' she whispered, almost holding her breath.

He turned to look at her at last, and for the first time she could see a kind of torture in his eyes. 'Because I'd convinced myself you didn't care what I believed. You hadn't tried to explain, you *told* me you'd lied to my mother—and then you walked away and took on Clover.'

A sensation akin to all the blood starting to run through her veins, as if it hadn't been before, as if she hadn't really been alive before, held her silent and stunned.

'And even a few minutes ago,' he said, 'you put down your nausea, looking traumatised and all the rest, merely to overwork. In other words saying it had nothing to do with me.'

She swallowed. 'I did lie to your mother,' she said barely audibly. 'She asked me if I'd fallen in love with you. I said no. But that was the only lie I told her.'

'Vivian—'

'No, Lleyton.' She put her hand over his. 'Let me finish. There were so many issues between us—not least the way you told me yourself you weren't for me—I…couldn't find a way through them but Ginny was the biggest, and I'm still not sure—'

'Ginny,' he interrupted, 'has gone out of my life for once and for all. And that happened,' he said, 'before I'd established with myself that I loved you.'

'But you said you would have stayed married to her—'

'I know, but only because of the child. And only to give that child a legitimate father, because I happen to believe children deserve it and I happen to believe they deserve to be born in wedlock, even though it may not last. But any other claim she thought she may have had on me, any hope she had of rekindling things couldn't have been more doomed when she chose to take up with Ralph, because she was showing her true colours again and—I didn't give a damn on my own account.'

Vivian frowned.

'Whereas,' he went on with an effort, 'when I thought *you* were dallying with Ralph I could have killed you both.'

She linked her fingers so the knuckles showed white in an effort to concentrate. 'But the night before we went to Palm Beach I thought you were—I knew you were upset, and that it was over Ralph and Ginny and that's why you needed to get away.'

'I was, but it was disgust, that's all.'

She thought for a few moments, then said a little helplessly, 'I still don't understand why you insisted I go to the ball.'

'At Palm Beach, the one thing I was affected by was you. It was like being assaulted on all fronts,' he said, with the first trace of humour in his eyes since he'd arrived. 'Deciding, after your painful declaration, that I couldn't continue with the deal—then finding myself kissing you.' His eyebrow quirked. 'But the *coup de grâce* came when you seemed to be able to put it all behind you, almost as if it had never happened. That's when, even although I'd done the breaking off, I suddenly found I couldn't let you go.'

Her lips parted incredulously.

'So it had nothing to do with Clover or Ginny—just you and I, Vivian.'

She put her hands to her cheeks as she felt the blood rush to them. And she said miserably, 'How was I to know that? I'd never have said the things I did…oh!'

'I know. It was all my fault. But the fact of the matter is, I haven't been thinking too straight since you walked into my office without your shoes. And, yes,' he said evenly, 'I was left with a legacy of bitterness and mistrust, so that I had no intention of letting any woman get too close, and I suppose my whole motivation for ever proposing that deal to you in the first place was to express my cynicism of women in general.'

'Why would I be able to change that?' she asked uncertainly. 'You walked in here hating me and…and all I stood for,' she said shakily.

'I walked in here hating the fact that I had fallen in love with you but you didn't seem to give a damn about me.'

She couldn't speak; she could only stare at him with all sorts of emotions flickering through her eyes. Then she got up and went over to the glass doors. The sun had set but the sky was still pink and gold with the radiance of it, and as she stared at it she didn't hear him get up. Then some intuition told her he was standing right behind her.

She half turned and said a little desperately, 'I did, but…' She stopped and sniffed. 'I really thought…I could mend things for you and Ginny at the ball, but it all blew up in my face. Then, when you left me the way you did—' She swallowed as he moved restlessly. 'I knew I could never trust you again, Lleyton. I…it couldn't have happened that way for me with a man without loving him, but I know it wasn't the same for you.'

'Vivian—'

'No,' she said very quietly. 'You didn't trust me then, when I let you look into my soul… I'm sorry, but I could never put myself there again. All right—' she gestured tiredly '—I am a bit of a wreck because of it, but I'll get over that in time. I could never cope with it again, though.'

'Do you honestly think you'd have to?' he said after an age.

She looked away.

'I'm not trying to downplay the things I did, but if you look at it from another angle you could see a different story.'

'No. I mean—'

'Vivian.' He made no move to touch her but she could see it was an effort. She could see a nerve beating in his jaw and an intensity in his eyes she'd never seen before, almost as if he was concentrating on a matter of life and death, and it shook her a little to see it. 'Do you think I'd be here now if I was still the same man you first met? If I was still disillusioned and looking for a kind of sensual challenge or, to put it more bluntly, a cheap thrill?'

Her lips parted.

He waited, taking in the rioting curls of her hair, her slim figure with her blouse still buttoned up crookedly, her white shorts and bare feet, her pale face.

Then he went on, 'Do you think I'd have allowed myself to care one way or another—do you *really* think I'd have let Ralph get to me over a girl who meant nothing to me? Would I be asking you to marry me when we've known each other for a month and spent three weeks of that month apart if I wasn't deadly serious?'

'Well,' she said helplessly, 'that is another thing. It was only a few days, really.'

'And yet,' he said barely audibly, 'after those very few days I knew I'd never be the same again. I knew I could never rest easy if I wasn't there…just to be there for you. In case of lifts, heights, planes, hiccups.' He closed his eyes suddenly. 'In case of some other man getting all the spirit and joy and sheer delight of Vivian Florey.'

'Oh…!'

He opened his eyes and said, not quite evenly, 'I could not bear the thought of another man making love to you, Vivian. And I can't visualise the rest of my life without you, except to know it would be hell.'

'Lleyton,' she whispered, then shook her head as if to clear her mind. 'Don't forget how much trouble I can get myself into…'

'Why do you think I love you so much?'

'That…that part as well?' she stammered incredulously.

'That part as well,' he agreed. 'I don't only want to go to bed with you, Vivian, I want to live by your side, I want to love you, laugh with you, protect you, have kids with you.'

She moistened her lips. 'What about the aircraft factory?'

'It can go to hell. It was only an excuse, anyway.'

Her eyes widened. 'You mean there isn't one?'

'No. There will be one one day, but it's only another business, whereas you, Vivian, would be my life and my pleasure.'

'So you'd never be bloody minded with me, and cross?' she asked.

He smiled down at her, and there was so much tenderness in his blue eyes she felt like fainting again. 'I can't promise that, and I'm pretty sure there'll be times when you might feel the same. So long as we know we're really soulmates…' He reached for her hand and looked deep into her eyes.

Vivian gave way wordlessly, and went into his arms as if she were coming home.

'It's all right. It's all right,' he said softly, kissing her hair and holding her close as she shook like a leaf in a storm. 'Trust me,' he said.

Nothing had ever felt so right for Vivian. Not only his strength and the sense of security she had in his arms but the feeling that she'd finally fused all the facets that Lleyton Dexter had shown her into one man, one much simpler entity, a man who loved her and all her phobias. It was like coming into a safe harbour at last, and she quietened gradually, then tilted her face to his. 'It's a funny thing, but at times I've never trusted anyone more.'

'It's a funny thing,' he repeated slowly, 'but I never knew what I was looking for until you came into my life. So sassy, feisty, *genuine* and… I can't put the rest of it into words, but I might be able to show you,' he said, and she felt the wave of pure feeling that ran through him as his arms tightened about her.

'I think I might be able to show you…how I feel about that,' she responded.

'You never told me,' Vivian said drowsily, and paused.

'What did I never tell you?' he prompted, and drew his hand down her naked body as they lay together on her bed, satiated and languorous in the aftermath of their love-making.

She smiled against his mouth, then leant her head on her elbow and looked down at him impishly. 'Perhaps because I feel thoroughly reached and squeezed, like a peach, although in the nicest not to mention an absolutely heavenly way—'

'I'm glad,' he interrupted, and with one swift movement he moved her to be lying on her back and eased his weight onto her.

'Lleyton,' she said severely, but her eyes were laughing.

'Do go on, Vivian.' But he started to lay a trail of feather-light kisses down her throat towards her breasts.

'Um...' she said with an effort. 'Yes, you never told me what you meant when you said that. About girls and peaches and trees.'

'Nothing.' He continued with his self-appointed task, which made concentrating extremely difficult for Vivian, especially with the way he touched and then teased her nipples with his teeth.

'Nothing?' She frowned.

'Well...' He lifted his head and his eyes danced with sheer devilry. 'It happened to be the quote for the day in my desk diary, and it occurred to me it might just get a rise out of you.'

'Lleyton Dexter,' she gasped, 'that's...!'

'Whatever you were going to say, I agree,' he said gravely. 'Diabolical, chauvinistic—but I'll tell you one thing, Vivian. That's when it first occurred to me that Julianna Jones might be drop-dead gorgeous but she couldn't hold a candle to you. I now know no one could, for me.'

Vivian trembled and sighed and took his face between her hands. 'I love you, Lleyton.'

'And I you, Vivian.' And he went on to make love to her in a way that saw them united in physical splendour and mental togetherness.

'What kind of a wedding would you like?'

They were in the lounge, in each other's arms on the settee, having showered, wearing their robes.

Vivian stirred and lifted her cheek from his chest. 'Oh! I forgot to ask you how it went!'

He looked down into her eyes. 'It went very well in the end. I gave Mag away to the man she loves, and all the drama and trauma of the lead-up melted away because she and Eddie were obviously so blissfully happy.'

'I'm so glad,' Vivian breathed. 'I would never have forgiven myself otherwise.'

He played with her hair. 'However, I'm inclined to agree with your first, rather scathing sentiments on the subject.'

Vivian smiled, but not so he could see. 'I take it, Lleyton, that means you're about to deny me a full week of festivities at the family estate and all the trimmings?'

'I just don't know if the family could stand it,' he said seriously. 'As it is my mother and Lady Wainright have fallen out, Ralph has taken himself off to Mexico and...' He paused. 'But if—'

She reached up and touched her forefinger to his lips. 'How about,' she said, with her eyes serious but the corners of her mouth quirking, 'a deserted island, Lleyton? Because I don't think I could go through another wedding week at Harvest Moon, either!'

He laughed and bent his head to kiss her. 'What say we compromise? A simple ceremony and lunch, perhaps at Palm Beach, no lead-up at all and only family. And then we could find ourselves a deserted island.'

'That sounds wonderful. When?'

'At the earliest possible date I can organise it,' he assured her. 'We'll need to look for a ring, and—'

Vivian sat up in the circle of his arms, her eyes wide.

'My darling,' he said quietly, 'this one we'll choose together. I'd hate to have you feeling in any way connected to a rent-a-girl.'

'Oh. But…well, I guess you could sell the other one. You did say it was a good investment,' she said.

'It was. Not any longer, however.'

'What do you mean?' She frowned as she visualised the pink diamond.

'It's sitting at the bottom of the Hawkesbury.'

'Lleyton!' she gasped. 'How come?'

'I threw it there, from the end of the jetty.'

Her lips parted incredulously. *'Why?'*

'Because it seemed to signify everything I'd done wrong since I laid eyes on you, Vivian. It seemed,' he said sombrely, 'to be the symbol of how I'd lost you.' He laid his head back and sighed. 'I'd taken it out one evening, determined to sell it. But I found myself at the end of the jetty, remembering how you'd fallen in—and it was like drowning.'

She smoothed the lapel of his robe and looked deep into his eyes.

'Everything we'd done together, said to each other, especially the way you'd made love to me, seemed to pass before my eyes,' he went on. 'And I discovered I hated that pink diamond with a vengeance, so I threw it in. But it only gave me momentary respite, because it was myself I hated. Then I felt guilty about wasting so much money, so I donated its worth to charity the next morning.'

'There's only one kind of ring that will mean anything to me,' she said softly. 'A wedding ring—a plain band. That's all. But I can't tell you how proud I'll be to wear it.'

'Sweetheart—'

'No, I mean it, Lleyton,' she warned. 'I never was a jewellery girl, remember? And I guess I'll always be...' She paused.

'There'll always be a bit of Vivian Florey in Vivian Dexter?' he suggested.

'I'm afraid so. Will you mind?' she asked directly.

'On the contrary, I'll be honoured,' he said simply.

And, true to her word, two weeks later she married him, in a filmy white dress, in the house at Palm Beach, with only family in attendance—although it included Stan and Isabelle Goodman and Lady Wainright, who had apparently made up her differences with Amelia Dexter.

Vivian wore flowers in her hair with the lovely but simple white dress, and the only ring she had on her left hand was a plain gold band. But her happiness, an almost ethereal radiance, was plain to see, causing Lleyton Dexter's mother to say to her oldest friend, who happened to be his godmother, 'I almost don't recognise him. He's like a different person.' She blinked strenuously as she watched Lleyton looking down at Vivian with his heart in his eyes.

'I always thought she had a lot of spirit,' Marlene Wainright murmured.

'Glory be,' Ralph muttered to his sister Mag, 'how the hell did Vivian achieve that?'

But Mag was laughing helplessly as she went forward to put her arms around her brother and his new wife.

* * *

When everyone had left, the bride and groom poured themselves a last glass of champagne and took it out onto the terrace. The day was sliding towards dusk and they leant on the railing with their arms around each other's waists.

'Thank you,' Vivian said, 'for a lovely wedding.'

'It was a pleasure, and you were the loveliest part of it.' He looked down at her meditatively for a long moment. 'And now I know you really trust me.'

'Well, I do, but…because I married you?' Vivian turned so they were facing each other.

'That too,' he conceded, and cupped her cheek with his free hand. 'But you wouldn't be standing here with me otherwise.'

Her eyes widened, and she looked down to see the sea boiling and roiling at the base of the cliff, but felt no fear. 'I never even thought about heights,' she said incredulously, then paused briefly before saying, 'Lleyton, you don't doubt that I love you, do you?'

'I sometimes wonder why, that's all,' he said after a long moment, and with something curiously searching in his dark blue gaze. 'I sometimes remember the things I said and did and don't know how you could forgive me…' He shrugged.

'It's simple,' she murmured, and went into his arms. 'You're my rock, my tree, my delight. And everything that happened along the way has fired my love and strengthened it into pure gold.'

'Oh, Vivian,' he said at last, after they'd stared into each other's eyes. 'I'm so glad you think so, because—I never thought I could love like this.'

'Neither did I,' she said shakenly, and clung to him as he started to kiss her deeply.

SEPTEMBER 2000 HARDBACK TITLES

ROMANCE™

One Husband Needed *Jeanne Allan*	H5284	0 263 16620 1
Delivered: One Family *Caroline Anderson*	H5285	0 263 16621 X
The Hired Fiancée *Lindsay Armstrong*	H5286	0 263 16622 8
Don Joaquin's Pride *Lynne Graham*	H5287	0 263 16623 6
The Pleasure King's Bride *Emma Darcy*	H5288	0 263 16624 4
The Truth About Charlotte *Lilian Darcy*	H5289	0 263 16625 2
The Wedding Deal *Janelle Denison*	H5290	0 263 16626 0
Sanchia's Secret *Robyn Donald*	H5291	0 263 16627 9
The Paternity Claim *Sharon Kendrick*	H5292	0 263 16628 7
Project: Daddy *Patricia Knoll*	H5293	0 263 16629 5
The Engagement Deal *Kim Lawrence*	H5294	0 263 16630 9
Their Convenient Marriage *Mary Lyons*	H5295	0 263 16631 7
Twice as Good *Alison Roberts*	H5296	0 263 16632 5
The English Bride *Margaret Way*	H5297	0 263 16633 3
The Determined Husband *Lee Wilkinson*	H5298	0 263 16634 1
His Very Own Baby *Rebecca Winters*	H5299	0 263 16635 X

HISTORICAL ROMANCE™

The Marriage Truce *Ann Elizabeth Cree*	H487	0 263 16868 9
An Innocent Masquerade *Paula Marshall*	H488	0 263 16869 7

MEDICAL ROMANCE™

Two's Company *Josie Metcalfe*	M405	0 263 16796 8
The Best Man *Helen Shelton*	M406	0 263 16797 6

SEPTEMBER 2000 LARGE PRINT TITLES

ROMANCE™

Title / Author	No.	ISBN
The Sheikh's Reward *Lucy Gordon*	1319	0 263 16700 3
Her Secret Pregnancy *Sharon Kendrick*	1320	0 263 16701 1
Marriage in Peril *Miranda Lee*	1321	0 263 16702 X
Bride On Loan *Leigh Michaels*	1322	0 263 16703 8
The Mistress Deception *Susan Napier*	1323	0 263 16704 6
The Unexpected Wedding Gift *Catherine Spencer*	1324	0 263 16705 4
A Wife at Kimbara *Margaret Way*	1325	0 263 16706 2
A Scandalous Engagement *Cathy Williams*	1326	0 263 16707 0

HISTORICAL ROMANCE™

Title / Author	ISBN
Miss Verey's Proposal *Nicola Cornick*	0 263 16880 8
The Elusive Heiress *Gail Mallin*	0 263 16881 6

MEDICAL ROMANCE™

Title / Author	ISBN
The Girl Next Door *Caroline Anderson*	0 263 16804 2
Dr Bright's Expectations *Abigail Gordon*	0 263 16805 0
Idyllic Interlude *Helen Shelton*	0 263 16806 9
An Enticing Proposal *Meredith Webber*	0 263 16807 7

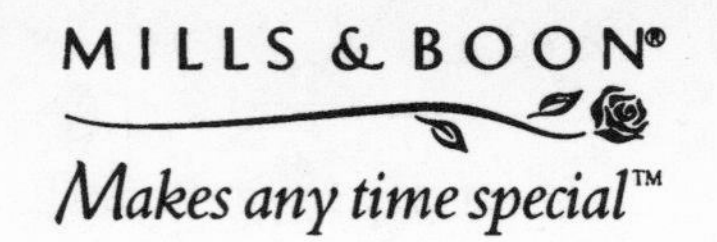

OCTOBER 2000 HARDBACK TITLES

ROMANCE™

Title / Author	Code	ISBN
A Most Passionate Revenge *Jacqueline Baird*	H5300	0 263 16636 8
Her Sister's Baby *Alison Fraser*	H5301	0 263 16637 6
The Christmas Child *Diana Hamilton*	H5302	0 263 16638 4
Wedding at Waverley Creek *Jessica Hart*	H5303	0 263 16639 2
Back in the Marriage Bed *Penny Jordan*	H5304	0 263 16640 6
The Baby Gift *Day Leclaire*	H5305	0 263 16641 4
Lisa's Christmas Assignment *Jessica Matthews*	H5306	0 263 16642 2
The Wife Seduction *Margaret Mayo*	H5307	0 263 16643 0
The Spanish Husband *Michelle Reid*	H5308	0 263 16644 9
In Love with the Boss *Doreen Roberts*	H5309	0 263 16645 7
Bride by Deception *Kathryn Ross*	H5310	0 263 16646 5
Gift-Wrapped Baby *Renee Roszel*	H5311	0 263 16647 3
A Bride for Christmas *Alexandra Scott*	H5312	0 263 16648 1
It Must Have Been the Mistletoe *Moyra Tarling*	H5313	0 263 16649 X
Worthy of Marriage *Anne Weale*	H5314	0 263 16650 3
Baubles, Bells and Bootees *Meredith Webber*	H5315	0 263 16651 1

HISTORICAL ROMANCE™

Title / Author	Code	ISBN
The Blanchland Secret *Nicola Cornick*	H489	0 263 16870 0
The Reluctant Puritan *Gail Mallin*	H490	0 263 16871 9

MEDICAL ROMANCE™

Title / Author	Code	ISBN
A Kind of Magic *Laura MacDonald*	M407	0 263 16798 4
Wrapped in Tinsel *Margaret O'Neill*	M408	0 263 16799 2